My Long Lost Amish Twin

Hannah Winstone

Published by Trellis Publishing, 2021.

MY LONG LOST AMISH TWIN

First edition. July 11, 2021.

ISBN: 979-8224931903

Written by Hannah Winstone.

MY LONG LOST AMISH TWIN

HANNAH WINSTONE

1

It was only eleven o'clock in the morning, the beginning of Rebecca Bartlett's shift, and already the pristine white halls were full to bursting. Doctors rushed past, nurses called to each other across the wide nurse's station - and most of all, patients demanded to be seen. There was never a break here, never a chance to sit down and think.

Already her patients list was growing; a man with a broken leg needed a scan, two sisters with the flu needed medication. Scanning down the page she saw another unrecognised person; Sarah Yoder. An unusual surname, but not the strangest she had ever seen. "what happened to her?" she questioned the Doctor that had handed her the new list. Already she was scanning the report, chocolate eyes skimming the page with expert precision.

"A car accident; hit and run. Someone found her unconscious by the road, but by the time the ambulance and police got there the car was already gone."

"Mmm." Rebecca flipped her clipboard closed, reaching across the nurse's station to grab a new pen. "I'll have a look at her now, sounds like it could be serious. It says here she has concussion."

"She still hasn't woken up. Doctor Akers is looking after her, but she'll need round the clock supervision just in case."

Rebecca nodded, stepping around the Doctor to start her rounds - but he grabbed her before she had the chance to take more than a single step. She turned to him, brow quirked in a silent question.

"There's one more thing," he started uneasily, "Originally she wasn't going to be on your roster, but we're understaffed. When you go in, don't be surprised."

"What do you mean?" Asking her not to be surprised only served to tell her there was a *reason* she might be. "I've been at this hospital for *years,* I've seen everything."

"Not *this,*" the Doctor replied with a huff, "have you ever seen your own doppelganger?"

Rebecca tugged her arm free, eyes snapping wide. What the hell did he mean by that? She regarded him for a moment, lips pursed - before spinning on her heels and marching down the crowded hall. Whatever he meant, Rebecca supposed she was going to find out very soon. Still, as she travelled down the hospital hall, she couldn't quite get his words out of her mind.

Sarah Yoder. Room 315. Sarah's slender hand hesitated on the door handle, dark eyes peering through the glass panel. It revealed nothing except for a dark haired woman with her head turned the other way. Sucking in a breath, Sarah entered.

She was still unconscious, that was obvious from her lack of reaction; but her breathing was stable, so that was something. Her chest rose and fell evenly, tiny hands relaxed by her side. As Sarah set her clipboard down and padded closer she noticed that the woman had gauze across her cheek, her lips dark and bruised.

Then she came to stand by the woman's side and her breath stopped. She blinked, then squeezed her eyes shut as if that might somehow clear her mind, allow her to see the truth. When her eyes flickered back open, the image was the same.

The woman lying in the bed, Sarah Yoder, was her own double. From the curve of her nose to the unusual broadness of her jawline, it was like looking in a mirror. Even through the bruising and the stitches it was clear; there was no denying it.

It was impossible to be mistaken; this woman was her *sister.* The sister she hadn't seen since she was a baby, the sister she didn't even remember save for what people had told her. Yes, Rebecca knew she was adopted, knew she had a twin - but while her sister had been brought up by the Amish community she was born in, Rebecca had been adopted by a lovely family in the centre of town.

Pursing her lips Rebecca leaned close. A strand of hair fell from its place tucked behind her ear and brushed across Sarah's cheek, She had a dash of freckles across her nose. It was one difference - and perhaps the only one - from Rebecca's own tanned but unmarked skin.

The door behind her creaked open, footsteps echoed across the tiled floor. Rebecca jumped, a small squeak escaping her lips, and whirled - but it was only Doctor Aker, the man in charge of Sarah's care.

"Uncanny, isn't it?" he questioned, voice hushed, "she looks just like you."

"She does," Sarah replied with a huff. Her heart was still hammering in her chest, her mind still a whirl of manic activity - but his entrance had snapped her back to her senses.

"Perhaps we shouldn't have added her to your patient roster; it must be strange." He ruffled his thick, greying hair, and offered her a smile. He didn't know about her past, couldn't know the thoughts rushing through Sarah's mind. "She came in last night and she's stable - but if she doesn't wake up soon it's going to be an issue." His eyes darted toward Sarah, thick brows creased in concern.

Rebecca shifted uneasily. She didn't know this woman, hadn't even *spoken* to her; and yet she felt an odd protectiveness swell in her chest. Stepping forward she said, "then we'll just have to do all we can for her and make sure she's all right."

Akers nodded, smiling. "We will."

Sarah chewed on her bottom lip, aware of the fact her lipstick was already gone but not really in the mood to care. "I still have rounds to do," she said with a forced smile, "but I'll come back and see to her."

As she left, Sarah cast a quick glance back to the unconscious woman in the bed, and shivered. Even as she turned down the hall to visit her next patient she couldn't get the image of Sarah's - and by extension, her own - bruised face out of her mind.

———————————————

Rifling through old records, both digital and traditional, brought up nothing about Sarah Yoder. Raised in a mostly secluded Amish community, Rebecca supposed if she was in good health she had never *needed* to visit a hospital. Still she had searched for hours, long after her shift had ended, and still turned up nothing.

So, plan B. Drive to the Sheriff's office and seek answers there. She should have waited until the morning instead of turning up at God knew what hour - but she found herself driving through town without even thinking. Before she knew it, Rebecca stood outside the Sheriff's office with her hands shoved deep in her coat pockets, staring at the firmly closed door like it held all of her answers.

Inside was warm, the rush of hot air a wonderful break from the freezing cold outside. It was almost empty save for the Sheriff himself, a younger man with a mop of dark hair and a broad build. His head snapped up from a tower of papers as she entered, his eyes squinted in confusion. "Ma'am?"

"Good evening. Or uh, night I suppose?" She shifted awkwardly, letting her eyes wander. Now that she was here it all seemed so *silly,* like the memory of Sarah was a million years ago. Almost like it had all been a dream. With a huff she snapped her attention back to the Sheriff. "I uh, I'm here about Sarah Yoder; the woman that was hit by a car last night."

His eyes widened in recognition. "Do you have information about the case?"

The word *case,* for some unknown reason, made her stomach squirm. It was more than just an accident, more than just something tragic and scary. It was *police business;* and she had no right to intervene. Yet her lips moved without permission as she said, "no, actually. I hoped you might be able to tell *me* what happened. I... I think she's my sister."

"You *think?*" The Sheriff - who's full name was Jacob Harris, according to his name tag - frowned. "I don't think I understand."

He sat behind a messy desk, and Sarah collapsed into the closest chair without thought. She had completed her hospital shift without complaint, eaten lunch in tense silence, and somehow driven here with herself intact. But now? It was like her energy had been sucked dry. "My name is Rebecca Bartlett," she started, "I'm adopted, I've known since I was a kid, and that woman looks *just* like me. She's Amish too, her file told me. My sister and I were born in the Amish community on the outskirts of town." It was too much coincidence, and her *features,* they were identical to Rebecca's own.

"So you want to know what *I know,* to confirm it all?" he surmised. Something clicked in him then, an acceptance of her circumstances. An understanding. The papers, long forgotten, were shifted out of the way so Harris could lean across the little desk. "I'll tell you this, Sarah's not the first to wind up dead or missing. Thirty years back, two women from that same community just disappeared. There have been more too, always women, who just vanish or are found dead miles away from where they live."

Rebecca shivered despite the heat. Her hands dug deeper into her pockets as she asked, "and you think Sarah is the latest victim?"

He shrugged. "We've never managed to pin anyone because the cause of death is never the same, and some women just never turn up. Still, I believe it's the same person, targeting Amish women."

All of a sudden Rebecca wished she hadn't asked, hadn't even *come here.* This was something she had no right to be involved in, something she didn't *want* to be involved in. Yet if Sarah really was her sister, didn't she owe it to her to help? Huffing out a sigh she leaned back, head tipping back. "Thirty years? It first happened thirty years ago and you've never caught anyone?"

"No. The case was closed, considered a dead end. There's something else, though - Sarah came to us last week, rushed in here all upset, crying. I could barely get a word out of her, but she said someone was after her."

"And you didn't *do* anything?" Rebecca gasped. Her head snapped up, eyes wide. Her chest hitched as she gazed at him.

"I thought she was crazy, but I offered help. Then she just ran off; I never even got her name. I recognised her when I was called to the scene yesterday."

Rebecca could have *slapped* him. Deep in her pockets, her fists clenched. No, that wasn't going to do anything except get her arrested. Running a hand down her face she asked, "have you been to her house? Investigated?"

"It's police business, out of Sheriff hands."

"Nonsense!" Tiny hands slammed against the wooden desk with enough force his papers jumped. He flinched himself, eyes wide. Without a care Rebecca demanded, "tomorrow you're going to look around, and I'm coming with you. She's my *sister,* and I'm not going to lose her before I even know her." Her eyes narrowed, a silent threat she didn't need to vocalise.

"I shouldn't take you with me," Harris stated - and then heaved a sigh, "but you don't seem like the type to take no for an answer. Meet me here tomorrow at ten o'clock."

Rebecca rose to her feet, unsteady and shaking but grinning with victory. "Thank you, Sheriff Harris," she replied with a smile, "I'll be there at ten exactly."

As she turned to leave she cast him one last smile - a genuine one, despite her uneasiness - and then the door swung open and she ventured back out into the cold autumn evening. This was only the beginning, and she didn't know what was going to happen next - but at least she was doing *something.* That at least made the tight knot in her stomach ease.

———————————————

The journey to Sarah's community seemed to take *forever.* Even though Sheriff Harris' car sped through town unhindered by so much as a red light - as at this time there was hardly any traffic along the route he chose - sitting in the front passenger seat, head bowed as she tried not to think about the day ahead, was *torture*.

At least the Sheriff was nice company - he spoke quietly, muttering quiet reassurances the entire time. He had insisted she call him by his first name too, but Rebecca still found herself referring to him simply as Sheriff.

By the time they pulled up to the outskirts of town, where the Amish community lived, Rebecca's entire body itched with the need to get out and investigate. She swung the car door open and climbed out before Harris had the chance to speak a word; but she at least took a moment to look around. Houses lined the left side of the street; simple buildings with neat little gardens and picket fences. To her right sat some kind of store; a bakery, she guessed by the pies in the window.

"We should take a look around," Harris spoke, springing Rebecca from her thoughts, "stay with me, please. You shouldn't even technically be here."

She simply pursed her lips and nodded. Harris took off down the road and Rebecca scampered after him. Despite the rising anxiety in the pit of her stomach she was almost giddy; finally, she might get some *answers*.

A group of woman stood by one of the houses, their curious gazes followed them as they walked. Not everyone that lived here was Amish, but their odd dresses and old fashioned hair told Rebecca those three women were. "Perhaps they'll know something?" she suggested.

"Perhaps. I'll talk to them," Sheriff Harris agreed. He smiled down at her - and Rebecca wasn't *short,* especially not in her heeled boots, but he towered above her. Rebecca found she didn't mind it at all.

They strolled up to the women, and Rebecca hung back to let Harris investigate. She wanted so desperately to interrogate them even for just a *sliver* of information; but she wasn't so stupid as to think that was a good idea. So instead she waited for Harris to start his questions, shoving small hands deep in her coat pockets.

"Good morning," Harris spoke, smiling softly, "My name's Jacob Harris, I figure you can tell my my uniform I'm the Sheriff. Could I talk to you lovely women for a few minutes?"

One woman quirked a brow, casting a glance between Harris and Rebecca. "Of course. What is this about?"

"Do any of you know a woman called Sarah Yoder? She's about thirty, dark haired; looks just like my friend here."

The first woman, red haired and older than the other two, glanced at Rebecca in a way that made her shiver. "Sure, I know Sarah. Her mother disappeared just after she was born. I was told her twin was adopted by a family in town, but Sarah stayed. I guess her father couldn't look after two children." She placed a hand against her heart, the sympathy so overbearing and so *fake* that it made Rebecca's skin crawl. "Has something happened to the poor woman?"

Harris and Rebecca shared a glance. "She was involved in a car accident; except we believe it *wasn't* an accident at all. Does anyone around here own a car? The witness said it was a grey 4x4, but didn't see the number plate."

One of the woman, a short lady with thick brunette curls, laughed. "Sir, we don't have cars. I'm afraid you're asking the wrong people."

The redhead huffed. "Well not everyone here is Amish. Elijah Shetler has a car; he comes from an Amish family but isn't Amish himself, although he is *very* involved in our community."

This was taking *too long*. Rebecca fidgeted, eyes snapping from one woman to the next. "And he has the right kind of car? Where does he live? We need to talk to him."

Sheriff Harris put a reassuring hand against her shoulder. His skin was warm even through the coat - but it had the desired affect. Rebecca untensed, shoulders slumping. "We can't just go around accusing people out of the blue," he muttered, "we have to have *reasons*."

The redheaded woman smiled, but it was uneasy. "I'd say talk to him. Didn't you know he was arrested thirty years ago? His wife disappeared, people thought he killed her."

The other two women shifted uncomfortably, their sneering smiles vanished. "What happened to his wife was *tragic,*" one said, "and he was never convicted. Leave the poor man alone."

"It was just talk," Redhead confirmed with a shrug, "but it's something to think about, is it not?"

Harris huffed a sigh. Rebecca knew there was no denying it any more; that was just the reason they needed to investigate this Elijah. He turned to her, eyes wary. "Let's go back to the office, we should have records of Elijah's arrest."

"Good, let's go back right now." Rebecca turned without so much as a thank you to the gossiping women, ready to march back to the car.

She only got two steps before Harris' gentle hand landed on her arm. Although he didn't try to pull her back with force it was enough to stop her in her tracks. "We might not find anything useful," he warned, "and for all we know this is nothing at all. Don't get your hopes up."

"I won't," Rebecca lied. Already she was bubbling with energy, eager to get out there and find who hurt her sister. She itched with newfound adventure.

Unconvinced, Harris let his hand slip from her arm with a heavy sigh.

Rebecca found she somewhat missed the reassurance of his heavy hand against her.

———————————————

Rebecca crept along in the darkness, eyes squinting as she carefully picked her way over rocks and fallen branches. She had parked at the side of the road, fearful of making the townspeople suspicious, and had made her way along the forest path instead. *Why* she had come alone, well after acceptable hours and intent on wandering through the neighbourhood she didn't know - but part of her simply couldn't stay away.

In truth, Rebecca didn't know where she was going. The path wasn't linear, and with no streetlights to lead the way everything looked identical; every tree the same as the last, every dip in the path just like the five before it. Although she might have started to realise what an awful idea this was, she was never one to give up. She certainly wasn't going to give up on her newly found sister, who was still all alone in the hospital ward.

Rebecca passed another towering tree, the same as the others that surrounded her - but something gave her pause. At the base of the tree sat an old photograph. It was surrounded by candles - candles that were long burned out, the wax discoloured with age. A shrine? A memorial to someone gone? Rebecca crouched in the dirt, ignoring how it clung to her jeans, and gently picked up the photograph. Fumbling for her flashlight, Rebecca investigated.

A man and a woman smiled back at her. The man was young, likely only a teenager; the woman looked the same age. Where the man wore a patterned shirt and long hair reminiscent of the seventies, the woman wore her hair pinned back beneath a kapp. Rebecca fumbled to take it from the frame - and on the back someone had written an anecdote. *Elijah and Grace, 1976.* Then underneath, writing that was clearly newer; *may you rest in peace my love. I'm sorry.*

Sorry. Sorry for what? Rebecca read it once, twice, and a third time - but the only thing that made sense was the name. Elijah. The man accused of murdering his wife. Was this mini altar created by Elijah for his deceased loved one?

It wasn't until Rebecca set down the photo that she noticed a second, smaller one almost hidden by the candles. This photo had no frame, weighed down by a piece of simple jewellery. A necklace. This one held the memory of a smiling woman in her early twenties holding two newborn children.

With a jolt of shock Rebecca *recognised* one child. A tiny birthmark on its leg, shaped like a cartoon-like cloud. It mimicked her own birthmark perfectly. Heart pounding in her chest Rebecca snatched up the photo, turning it over in shaking hands.

Barbara and the twins, it read, *1981.* Then underneath, much like the first photograph, *rest in peace, and may your children join you soon.* The next part had been scratched out, almost incomprehensible in the darkness - but Rebecca just made out enough to send a chill down her spine. *I never meant to hurt you, but it had to be done.*

Those children, they were Sarah and Rebecca. The woman, Barbara... her mother? Her head *spun* as she lurched to her feet, dropping the photograph with a gasp. Elijah, he had killed his wife, killed her mother too. But why was there an altar in the middle of the woods, hidden from everyone? Why was there a photograph if *her mother* in an altar for Elijah's dead wife?

Was Elijah her father?

Rebecca reeled back, her head spinning - and when her foot caught on the uneven ground she went tumbling down back to earth. Her back struck the cold ground and she saw *stars.* All thoughts of visiting the town vanished.

The pain creeping up her back brought her snapping back to reality. She struggled to kneel, brushing dirt from her coat, and let her eyes wander to the ground she had so stupidly tripped over. It was raised, a lump of uneven earth both longer and wider than herself. If she hadn't known better she might have said it looked like... an old grave.

Her eyes snapped from the earth to the altar, then back again. Without allowing herself time to think she stood, faced the way she had come, and marched back to her car. She had a shovel in there and she *had* to know.

Rebecca returned half an hour later, shovel held in her shaking hands. *It's just uneven ground,* she tried to reason, *happens all the time in forests.* It was stupid to think this was *real.* It was her own paranoia, the darkness making everything spookier and stranger than it really was.

Yet she couldn't help it. Her body moved on autopilot as she struck the dirt with the shovel, small body straining to toss the dirt aside. With each fresh scoop of dirt her chest hammered louder, her pulse raced faster, and her stomach dropped further. Somehow, despite her own attempts at reasoning, she knew there was something here.

Something that she didn't *want* to see.

Minutes ticked on, and those minutes slowly stretched to an hour. Then two. Rebecca dug further and further into the earth until, finally, she couldn't dig any more. Sweating, she discarded her coat and collapsed onto the ground with a low groan. Rebecca wiped a dirty hand across her forehead, grabbing for her flashlight. She hadn't found a *damn thing* and now she felt so stupid - but she had to check. Just to make sure.

When she shone the blue tinted light into the hole, her heart shuddered. Yellow-white chunks stood out against the dark earth, poking out from the darkness. *Bones.*

Completely by accident she had just discovered a hidden grave.

Rebecca toppled back with a cry, her heart skipping painfully in her chest. Her mind raced, but she didn't dare look back down there. Suddenly she needed to leave, needed to run and never look back. Her skin itched from the dirt, dirt that had been hiding bodies, and she wanted to be sick.

Yet she needed to be sensible. Delicate hands shook as she scrambled for her phone, still scooting away from the grave. The dial tone droned on an on and for one horrible moment she thought Harris wouldn't pick up.

Then his voice, so warm and soft and *reassuring,* asked, "yes, who is this?"

"Rebecca Bartlett. You need to come here immediately. I found something... something *awful.* I, I think I found my mother's body."

Silence, and then, "I'm on my way. Don't move."

———————————————

Sleep didn't come easily for Rebecca; in fact, it hardly came at all. By the time she made her way to the Sheriff's office the next day she was little more than a zombie working on autopilot. She collapsed into the nearest chair with a groan, barely lifting her head when Harris asked if something was wrong. "Nothing," she replied, not too convincingly, "just tired. I kept thinking about that grave *all night.*"

He hummed sympathetically, reaching out a hand to sweep stray hair from her eyes. "Maybe this will cheer you up," he replied, sifting through a stack of old paperwork. After a moment he plucked a folder from the pile and slid it across the desk. "Elijah Shetler's original arrest back in the eighties."

That perked her up. Rebecca shot up in her seat, eyes wide as she scooped up the bundle of papers. Without prompt she began to read, drinking it all up.

According to the file his wife went missing in February of nineteen eighty-two, just two months after the disappearance of Barbara Yoder. Although he was eventually let off due to insufficient evidence, there were at least a handful of people that believed he was responsible.

"That isn't all," Harris murmured, "have a look at these files too."

Rebecca did, and her heart dropped as she moved from one file to the next. Elijah's wife, Rebecca's mother, two young cousins nearly half a dozen other women had all either gone missing or been found dead in the last thirty years. All of them from the same Amish community.

"Every single one of these woman is connected to Elijah somehow. His wife is obvious. The two young women were neighbours, and according to testimonies he showed romantic interest in at least one of them."

"What about Barbara - my mother?" It was still strange to call her such; she had died long ago, when she was just a baby. Nose crinkling, Rebecca shoved the files away.

"She was married to an Amish man, but was in a relationship with Elijah in secret. Not a very well kept secret, obviously; its in her file."

Shit. Her eyes snapped up, wide and beginning to glisten with tears. No, impossible. Her chest lurched, hands trembled. "Do you think... could Elijah be my father? Do you think Sarah knew?"

Harris' warm hand closed around her own, a gentle smile spreading across full lips. "I doubt it; Elijah and Grace never had kids of their own; and according to medical records Elijah *couldn't.*"

Relief. It washed through her, wiping her mind clean. *That,* at least, was a little comfort. "Thank God."

Harris smiled; and Rebecca smiled back, the first *genuine* smile in days. She was lucky to have him; to have him trying to solve this crime, to have him by her side, to have his support and affection. Because that's what it was, really; affection. Neither had ever said it aloud but that didn't make it less *true.*

They sat quietly, hands still intertwined, and Rebecca couldn't force herself to look away. Had his eyes always been so dark, so gorgeous? Had his smile always been so *sweet?* Perhaps she had just been too busy, too lost in thought, to ever notice - but she noticed *now,* and he truly was handsome.

Rebecca cleared her throat as she snatched her hand back, shoving her chair back to scramble away. "We should arrest Elijah. This is how it works, right? We have evidence now." She turned too quickly, tripping over the leg of the heavy wooden chair, but didn't even pause to right herself.

She was reaching for her coat when Harris stopped her, thick hand against her shoulder. "Wait." It wasn't a demand but a request, barely loud enough to hear.

Rebecca turned, cheeks burning, lips parted in question - but she never had the chance to voice her thoughts. Soft lips against her own, warm and tasting vaguely of coffee. Her eyes snapped wide; but as Harris - no, *Jacob* - tugged her closer her eyes fluttered closed. Rebecca could have *lost* herself in him, in those soft lips and his thick body against her own.

They parted with a breathy sigh, Rebecca's cheeks flushed crimson. Jacob simply grinned at her, almost *smugly,* and ran a hand through her hair. "I know this case is personal for you," he started, breathless himself, "but you need a break. You'll wear yourself out."

"If that's what it takes," she answered, "but I have to admit that was... kind of amazing." Rebecca snorted at her own ridiculousness. She wasn't some lovesick teenager, for goodness sake! Still, it was true.

"Then if you won't take a break, perhaps we can go out when this is all over? You deserve it, after all this."

A laugh bubbled in her throat and she swallowed it down. "That sounds nice," she replied simply. Honestly she wanted nothing more than to forget about this, if just for a few hours, and spend the day with him; but there were more important matters. She just hoped they could put it behind them. Soon.

Jacob leaned down to sweep another kiss across her lips, smiling against her soft skin, and curled a lock of her dark hair around his finger. "If you're ready, let's go."

"I am," she replied with a nod, "let's get our killer."

———————————

It had only been a handful of days since they had last visited, but it felt like a million years ago since they had first rolled up to the little Amish community. It looked the same as she remembered, with the little houses and cheerful shops; it was *Rebecca* that was different.

This time they didn't stop to talk to curious onlookers; with Elijah's address burned into their memory they marched right up to his door.

Although she wanted nothing more than to rush in there Rebecca stood back, behind Jacob, allowing him to take the lead. Even so she stood on her toes to peek over his shoulder.

The man that opened the door was in his fifties, beginning to grey around the sides even though his beard was still totally black. It was impossible not to see the resemblance to the young man in the grainy photograph that stood by the makeshift shrine in the forest.

"Elijah Shetler?"

"Yes. Is there something wrong?"

Jacob's lips pursed as he nodded. "Yes, and you're coming with us." He stood tall as he reached for the handcuffs hanging on his belt, not wavering even as Elijah stumbled back in shock. "I'm arresting you on suspicion of murder. The police are on their way."

Rebecca tuned out the rest. She had expected Elijah's arrest to bring about some satisfaction, some kind of relief, but none of that happened. She still didn't know *why* her mother was dead, why he had killed so many innocent women. Why he had tried to kill *Sarah*. She stumbled back as Jacob wrestled with Elijah; she darted down the steps, trying to block out his shouts and the whispers of curious neighbours.

"I knew it was him all along," one man called, "he killed his wife, didn't he? And he hit that poor girl with his car!"

"Don't be ridiculous," a woman scoffed. She didn't even *attempt* to hush her voice. "Why would Elijah hurt that lovely woman?"

Elijah grunted as he was shoved down the porch steps. They had quit struggling, Elijah having clearly decided it wasn't worth trying to fight someone twice his size. He glared at Rebecca as he stormed past - and then his eyes widened. "You look just like Sarah. Who are you?"

"Her twin sister," Rebecca snapped, "Barbara's daughter."

Elijah paused, eyes snapping between Jacob and Rebecca as if considering his options. There was something unnatural about the wideness of his eyes, the stillness of his body. "She deserved what she got, you know," Elijah growled, "it's a shame she survived. No one else did."

Rebecca spluttered, lost for words as her mind *spun*. "You *did* do it!"

He paled. As if his eyes weren't wide enough they widened further; it would have been comical if it wasn't so *frightening*. "No, I never - I didn't say that."

"Why'd you hurt her? Why did you kill my *mother?*"

Behind them more neighbours had gathered, standing in a gaggle right by the fence. They whispered among themselves, and Rebecca thought if they owned phones or cameras they would have probably tried to record it all. Why couldn't people just mind their own business?

"Come on, move it," Jacob insisted as he pushed Elijah forward - but Rebecca stopped him.

"No, I want to know what he has to say."

Elijah's lips peeled back and for a heart stopping moment she thought he was going to throw himself at her - but he only lurched forward, pretending to. "She deserved it too. I *loved her,* but she loved her stupid husband more. Grace wanted to *leave me* when she found out - but I wouldn't let her. Everyone leaves me in the end, so I did what I had to do to keep them with me."

Rebecca's hands shook, her heart thundered so loudly in her chest she thought she might pass out. "*Killing people* doesn't keep them with you! You can't destroy a life because you're *jealous.*" She marched forward, fire in her eyes, and shoved Elijah with every ounce of strength in her tiny body. "What about the others, huh? You killed *half a dozen* other people. Why?"

"They betrayed me too," she snarled, "just like Grace and your *mother,* they tried to leave. They found out too much or they got bored, it doesn't matter *why*. It had to happen. God willed it."

That was *enough*. Rebecca turned away, fists clenched so hard her knuckles began to ache. "If you think God willed you to kill women just because of petty *jealousy,* then prison is too good for you."

"You know, Sarah figured it all out. She found the altar I left for my two loves, pieced it together herself. You're both smart women, but her arrogance nearly got her in the end."

Rebecca bit down on her lip to keep from crying out. Across the streets the neighbours gawked, gossiped, but it didn't matter. They had a *real* confession, something undeniable, and she finally knew what had happened.

"Stick him in the car," she murmured - and Jacob was all too happy to comply.

She watched from a distance as Jacob manhandled him into the back of the Sheriff's car, slamming the door with enough force the entire car rocked on its wheels. Distantly police sirens wailed, signalling their approach.

It was all over.

Rebecca would have collapsed if Jacob's strong arms hadn't pulled her against his warm chest. She buried her face in his uniform, not caring for the whispers of the onlookers, and breathed in the smell of coffee that always clung to him.

"It's over," he whispered, "and Sarah is safe."

"Thank you," she murmured back, reaching up to kiss the corner of his lips, "you've no idea how much this means to me." She peppered more kisses along his cheek, his forehead, before finally settling against his lips.

"So," he muttered against her lips, "how about that date?"

She might have laughed, but there was simply no energy left. "Honestly I'd rather just go home, watch a bad movie to take my mind off of things." She paused, flickering up to meet his soft gaze. "Would... would you stay with me? Just for tonight; I don't think I want to be alone."

Jacob nestled a hand in her tangled hair, his smile gentle. "Of course. If that's what you want, I'll never leave your side."

"I'd love that," Rebecca replied tiredly; and she *meant* it.

THE AMISH LOVE OF CLAIRE MILLER

Claire Miller was a simple woman; she wanted to live her life how she saw fit, make her own decisions - and, most importantly, have control over her own life. It wasn't, she thought, an absurd thing to ask.

Unfortunately, her father didn't feel the same. He had controlled the family since long before she was born; and since her mother's death three years ago it had only become *worse*. It was stifling, overwhelming, and sometimes so much Claire felt as if she could barely *breathe* without unwanted criticism. It wasn't as if she wanted to abandon their way of life; she just wanted a little more autonomy.

Which is why she sat in their dimly lit living room with a book on her lap, studiously ignoring her father - *and* her sister Susannah - as they went on and on about their latest obsession; finding Claire a husband.

"You're old enough now you should have been married years ago," Susannah stated with a small huff. She crossed thin arms across her chest, staring down at Claire through narrowed hazel eyes. "I married Caleb five years ago and we're *almost* the same age"

Claire turned the page of her book, eyes flickering up to Susannah for only a moment before dipping back down. She had lost her place in the story three pages ago but she kept her gaze even. The last thing she wanted was for her family to know they were getting to her. She could just imagine the satisfaction in Susannah's slender face if Claire snapped.

"We only want what is best for you," her father commented softly. He was being unusually gentle today - trying a new approach? He had to have known by now that giving her orders would never work. "The older you become the less chance you have. Our community is small, and there aren't many men of marrying age."

"Perhaps," she stated calmly, closing the book and turning a cool gaze to her father, "I simply don't *want* to get married. Marriage isn't everything you know."

His lip curled, eyes flickering to Susannah as they shared a look of mutual discomfort. When he took in a breath it was uneasy and she knew he was trying to stay calm. "Claire dear, you must understand how important this is for you-"

"For *me?*" she replied, voice rising. He *was* getting to her, as he always did, and she hated it. "Best for *you,* you mean? You have never once cared about what I want or how I feel - if you did, you might have more sympathy toward me."

"I know you don't think finding a suitable man is worth your time but you just need to give it a chance. There aren't many available men, but if you *tried,* you would find someone interested." Susannah - who was considered the beautiful one in the family, and for good reason - only cared about two things; raising children, and interfering in Claire's life. Perhaps it was because she *pitied* Claire, believing her disinterest in finding a husband was some deep-rooted fear of rejection.

It wasn't, but it certainly seemed like something Susannah would believe.

"I don't want a husband. I have more worth than as a wife, and there's plenty I want to do before I settle down." Heaviness settled deep in her gut, but there was a fire building in her chest. "It's only your own reputations you care about-"

"We care about *you.* If you weren't moping around the house all the time and actually *met* someone-"

"I don't *mope!*" Claire's indignant cry was followed by a huff and her hands clasped so tightly around the book her knuckles turned pale white.

"You do," her father replied, "your mother died *three* years ago, and it's about time you put it behind you."

That was *enough*. Claire rushed to her feet and the book thudded to the ground as it tumbled from her lap. Her chest heaved with deep breaths as she kicked it aside. "You know Mother has *nothing* to do with this! How dare you use her for your own agenda?" Delicate hands clenched into fists and she just wanted to *grab* something, to hurl it across the room. Instead she settled for snatching a cushion from the sofa and throwing it at her father.

It hit his face with a dull thud before dropping listlessly to the floor. Although his face twisted, thick brows dropping low over his eyes, he said nothing. His glare was enough to make most people cower.

Susannah's features morphed into a wide eyed stare, a hand raising to cover her mouth.

"Don't bother saying anything," Claire snapped, "I'm going for a walk."

With that she whirled, storming past the book and the abandoned cushion and reaching blindly for the door. She flung it open and marched into the hall, chest swelling with that unfamiliar flame.

The living room door slammed shut behind her, echoing through the little hall and rattling in her ears. Then there was only silence.

Claire stood there for a moment, lips pursed as she tried to calm her erratic breathing. It left her lungs in short puffs, chest heaving beneath her loose navy dress. Eventually it calmed, but still too loud in the tiny hallway.

A walk. That was what she needed. It was too warm for a coat but she grabbed one without thinking as she marched past the coat hooks adorning the wall. Then the front door creaked open on old, unoiled hinges and she stepped into the warm spring air.

She stood there for a moment taking in the soft breeze and the rustle of the leaves - until something black and fluffy streaked past her legs. In a flash it bounded down the porch steps with a cheerful bark, and then disappeared down the little cobbled path leading past the street.

Oh no. *Oh no.* Belle! Her father had always warned her to be careful of letting their collie out - and she hadn't even thought to check before opening the door. Claire's heart jumped into her throat and for a moment she could only stare after the disappearing bundle of fur. Then with a gasp that caught in her throat, she sprinted after her.

A herding dog at heart, Belle was far too quick for Claire's short limbs and the thick dress that caught around her legs. Not to mention the coat that clung to her, sweltering in the heat as the sun beamed down. The breeze pulled loose strands of dark hair and she grabbed for the kapp that threatened to fall from her head.

She reached the end of the path and there was no dog in sight. She had left her community now, reaching the border of trees that signified the modern world beyond. Now, Claire considered herself an intelligent woman and she wasn't so sheltered that she had never left the spread of land she called home - but even so she hesitated.

Until she saw Belle plopped on someone's lush green garden, head tilted to the side as if to say *come and get me.*

"I swear," Claire muttered, "if I didn't love you so much I'd just leave you out here." Her gaze honed in to Belle as she stepped over. Everything else melted away until it was just her and Belle, irritation rising as she watched the dog patiently wait across the road.

Belle let out another cheerful, oblivious bark as Claire knelt beside her. Claire rolled her eyes and pressed a quick kiss between Belle's ears.

"Are you all right?"

Claire let out a shriek - one so undignified she was just thankful no one she knew was around to hear it. When her eyes snapped up she was met with a handsome, blond haired man wearing a baseball cap. He smiled, revealing perfect white teeth and... some kind of tongue piercing? The concept baffled her.

"Miss?"

"Uh." Great, as if she hadn't embarrassed herself enough. Claire's cheeks flushed as she scrambled to her feet, dress tangling about her ankles as she tried to stand. "I'm fine! Perfectly all right. I uh... just had some trouble with my dog." As if to prove a point she glared down at Belle - who only barked in response. Of course. "I'm terribly sorry! Is this your garden?"

It had only just occurred to her that the man had appeared from the house holding garden tools she barely recognised. She also noticed, dimly, that the grass around them had been all but destroyed by Belle's over eager claws and love for digging. Oh dear.

But still the man smiled, and when he shrugged he seemed so genuinely unconcerned it gave her pause. "It's nothing I can't fix, so don't worry about it. If your dog okay?"

Claire simply nodded.

The man seemed relieved. "Good. I have a dog too, I know what it's like when they run off. Oh, here she is now."

As if on cue a tiny French bulldog peeked from between his legs, pink tongue sticking from her mouth. She was *adorable,* so small and sweet with those big ears.

"She's lovely!" Claire announced, delighted - and for a moment her worries just washed away.

"Her name is Beatrice - my sister named her, not me."

Claire didn't see why it mattered - Beatrice was a *lovely* name - so she simply smiled. "This is Belle - my mother named her." Mother had named all of their pets since Claire was a baby; but she wasn't alive to name them any more. It was the only thing keeping Claire from getting a second dog - not that this man needed to know any of this.

This man... oh, she didn't even know his name!

"I must apologise; I never introduced myself." Here she was, intruding on his property and she didn't even tell him her name. "My name is Claire; Claire Miller." She smiled bashfully and raised a hand to wave - only to drop it without bothering. Could she *be* any more awkward?

"Ethan Brady. It's nice to meet you, Claire."

She flushed darker - and beside her Belle let out a bark as if to draw further attention to them both. Frankly she was surprised Belle hadn't tried to run off again, but she wasn't complaining. Especially if her staying here meant she had the chance to talk to Ethan more.

"You must live nearby, right?" Ethan questioned as he padded down the porch steps. He set the box of tools off to one side, then scooped up Beatrice with ease. She wiggled in his grasp, but then settled her head against his elbow quite happily.

It was such a *cute* sight that Claire melted. She almost forgot he had even asked her a question - until she registered his expectant look. He must have thought she was so strange; and not just because she was Amish. "I do, yes. I uh, live in the little Amish community nearby. There isn't many of us, though."

He smiled - and for a moment it seemed almost *wistful.* "It must be great, living in such a tight knit community. This town is so big and everyone's so busy; it's difficult to really get to know people." He frowned for a moment - and then shrugged as if to physically dispel those thoughts. "Would you like to come in for a while? I was just about to make lunch. Do you like soup?"

Claire blinked, cheeks flushing so brightly they *burned.* It was different for him - inviting someone for lunch was no more unusual than talking to them in the street. "I'm afraid it isn't appropriate for me to do so; but thank you."

"Oh, of course!" This time she swore *he* flushed; but perhaps it was just the heat. "I didn't think, sorry. I suppose I should let you get back home, now you've found your dog."

"I should be going, yes." She didn't want to imagine how angry Father was going to be when she returned. Perhaps she just wouldn't mention Belle at all. Claire glanced up, eyes lingering on Ethan for a moment. Had his eyes always been so startlingly blue? Then she looked down and her eyes landed on the mess at her feet. "I'm sorry for ruining your garden."

"It's no trouble, honestly," he replied with a laugh, "don't worry about it."

"I should at least pay for the damage or something." Her lips curled, eyes narrowed in thought.

"Please, don't worry. Although," he paused as if considering his words, "if you wanted, you could come back tomorrow and help. I could do with another pair of hands."

It wasn't appropriate - and her father would be so angry if he found out. So she said the only sensible thing.

"I would love to."

———————————————

Claire did her best to avoid her father the next day - and Susannah, and her other three sisters. She knew exactly what talking to them would result in and had no desire to start another argument. Besides, there were other things on her mind.

Such as Ethan. She would never admit it aloud, especially not within earshot of family, but there was just something about him she couldn't stop thinking about. And then there was his offer to come back... it was a kind request born of the desire for friendship, but Claire knew her father would hardly see it that way.

Which is why she stood on the little cobbled path with a basket in her hands, willing herself to move but unable to do so. It was just a ten minute walk to Ethan's street and it was such a simple journey; yet her feet froze and all of a sudden her body weighed a tonne. Just sliding one foot in front of the other seemed impossible.

The longer she stood there debating, the more difficult it would become to leave. Claire sucked in a deep breath and let her eyes slip closed, mentally willing herself to just *walk*. She would only be an hour, there and back before her father noticed. A smile crossed her face then, and she took a step forward with new resolve.

After that, there was a spring in her step not there before.

Claire, with the basket swinging cheerily by her side, made it to the end of the path in record time. Before she knew it she was looking across the street at Ethan's pleasant little house and his lovely garden. His car was there, as well as some big hulking machine she knew to be a motorbike. It rested against the closed garage door, and Claire found herself eyeing it warily as she approached to knock on his front door. It looked *dangerous;* why did people enjoy using them?

Her knock was light, hesitant, but after only a beat the door opened to reveal Ethan. He wore a red shirt the shade of sunsets, sleeves rolled up to reveal tanned arms - much more interesting than her plain grey dress and the thick stockings she always wore despite the weather. A look of confusion crossed his face for a moment - and then he beamed. "Claire! I wasn't sure if you would actually come back."

Her eyes widened. "I'm sorry! If you're busy, I can leave."

"No, I was hoping I would see you again." He smiled, so genuine and warm and unlike the sour expression of most men she knew. "Would you like to come in, or is it still inappropriate?"

Hesitation. Claire was sure he meant well but even so; their lives were so different, so contrasted, and she doubted he realised just how *terrible* an idea it was for someone of her culture. So she shook her head no and tried to ignore the disappointment settling in her stomach. "Thank you, but I would rather stay out here. Anyway, isn't the weather so warm today? Oh!" She paused, lifting the basket and peeling back the covering. Inside sat an array of treats; pastries and biscuits, as well as freshly grown fruit from her sister's orchard. "These are for you. Think of it as an apology for yesterday."

His eyes widened, that lovely smile growing - even as he shook his head in what might have been embarrassment. "Thank you, that's sweet. You coming back is enough, but these do look delicious."

"I don't eat sweets much, but I thought we could enjoy them while we work on your garden - if you would like to, of course." *He* had invited *her,* but this was so surreal and for a moment she wondered if he wanted her there at all. It surely must have looked odd to the neighbours. What if he had just been polite?

His beaming smile and the gentleness as he took the basket told her he was genuine. He really was handsome, with his messy blond hair and dimples when he smiled. Even that odd tongue piercing wasn't so bad when paired with his grin. Not that she was thinking about it, of course. His attractiveness was just... an observation.

No, who was she kidding? This man had captured her heart in only a day - and there was nothing she could have done.

"Claire?"

She blinked, eyes darting up to meet his. "I'm sorry?"

His laugh was light, pleasant, and Claire shivered. "I asked if you would like a drink."

"Oh." She blinked again, and suddenly it was as if she had forgotten how to form words. The breeze rustled at the hem of her dress, unsteadied the kapp from her hair and it occurred to her just how out of place she was. She took in a breath but it did nothing to help - instead she only felt sick.

"Claire, are you okay?"

"Fine," she replied too quickly, the words tumbling from her lips, "but I have to go."

"Already? You just got here-"

"I know, and I apologise. Goodbye, Ethan."

Not even a second passed before she spun, boots clinking against the path, and all but ran from his house. Her cheeks burned, her eyes dampened, but she didn't dare look back.

———————————————

"Claire dear, we *know* you don't enjoy us bringing up the subject but my husband thinks one of his cousins might be interested in meeting you-"

"Absolutely *not*." Claire stood in the kitchen with a rag in her hands, angrily scrubbing at the dirt-caked oven. She had steadily been working away for half an hour, quite peacefully, and now here was Susannah and Father *again*. So much for avoiding them.

"Claire, I'm starting to become bored of your refusal to cooperate. Do you want to be unmarried forever?"

The rag fell from her hands as Claire rose to her feet. Although she stared down her father evenly she felt her stomach churn and her heart lurch at the narrow eyed look he cast her. She shifted from one foot to the next. "No, but do you honestly believe you're helping me by trying to force me into marriage?"

"Yes," he replied simply. Then his voice lowered, almost a growl. "You need to start thinking about your future instead of living in the past. Your mother isn't here to defend your choices any more."

Claire's intake of breath rattled in her chest and it seemed to *echo* in the silent kitchen. "Perhaps I will get married; but it won't be to anyone of *your* choosing. I don't care if it's tradition." The words tumbled from between her lips then, bursting from her without thought or care. He *needed* to know that she didn't belong to him. "I will marry whomever I please - and perhaps it won't even be someone you know. Perhaps I'll marry Ethan-"

"Who's Ethan?"

Her lips clamped shut and her chest seized. Hazel eyes widened and this time her gasp was so tiny it was barely a sound. "Ethan?" she squeaked.

Susannah's lips parted - but no words left her. This was the first time she had *ever* been stunned into silence and Claire's blood went cold knowing it was her that caused it.

"You know a man named Ethan? Have you been talking to someone behind my back, leaving the house and the community to talk to strange men?" Her father, a tall and broad shouldered man, dominated the tiny space and Claire suddenly felt so small.

But still she kept her head high. "I have made a friend, that's all; but if I would like us to be more then that is *our* decision and not yours."

She ignored her sister's gasp and held her ground - but the prick of tears at the corner of here eyes was undeniable.

When her father spoke, Claire froze. "If you want to be with someone, I can't stop you," he said, so frighteningly calm and unlike himself, "but if you do, I don't want you coming back. This won't be your home any more."

"Father-"

Claire had no time to hear Susannah's words - whether defence or agreement for her father's words she had no idea. The sound drowned out until nothing was left - and then Claire fled from the kitchen, shoving past them both with a sob caught in her throat.

By the time she had fled the house and sprinted down the path, Claire realised where she was running. Ethan's house. She almost tripped over her dress as she stumbled up his driveway - only to hesitate with her fist against the door. This was *ridiculous*. They barely knew each other and there was no way he was interested in her the same way she liked him. Aside from that, he surely didn't want a crying woman on his doorstep. Leave. She had to leave-

Suddenly the door cracked open and there stood Ethan, his little dog Beatrice peeking her head from between his legs. His eyes locked with hers and for a moment they just stared silently at each other - until Ethan's broad arms swept her into a tight embrace. "I don't know what happened," he said with a sigh, "but I can tell it was bad. Come inside and tell me about it."

This time Claire didn't refuse - she followed him inside without a word, letting him coax her into the living room and into a plush leather armchair. She accepted the glass of water he offered without a word. It wasn't until he settled down on the sofa across from her that she realised he had been talking the entire time.

"I'm sorry," she amended, wiping her eyes with the hem of her sleeve. She wasn't even crying, not really - just allowing silent tears to roll down her cheeks.

"Don't apologise," Ethan assured with a kind smile - the kind of smile that lit up her chest and even squeezed a smile of her own from her lips. "What happened?"

"My father he... he wants me to get married but I told him no. Then today I said something so *stupid,* and I think he threatened to disown me." Her pale hands tightened around the glass. She stared at the water sloshing around inside, staring blankly as a drop splashed onto her dress. Finally she sighed and revealed, "I told him about *you.*"

"Me?"

No. He didn't need to know how she felt, he didn't need that kind of pressure. So she kept quiet, pursing her lips as if to physically withhold the words desperate to spill out.

"Claire?"

That simple word, that *one* use of her name with such softness and concern almost broke her. She blinked back more tears and sucked in a breath - but she couldn't hold it in. "I told him I had feelings for you. I know it's silly and I shouldn't have, and I know you don't feel the same-"

"Is it true?"

"What?" Blurry eyes turned to Ethan, lips parted and cheeks flushed.

"Is it true, that you have feelings for me?"

"Yes." She sighed, head dropping. A strand of hair fell from her kapp but she ignored it, simply letting it drop in her eyes. "I'm sorry, I should never have said anything."

"Hey." Ethan inched closer - although his distance was still respectable. Even so she saw him fighting with himself, torn between wanting to comfort and not knowing how. "Do what feels *right.* If your father isn't letting you be who you want to be, that's on him. Besides," he winced, as if his own words caused him embarrassment, "maybe I like you too. It's only been a few days but... I feel like we have something. Something I can't describe."

Claire let a laugh tumble from her lips and she flushed so scarlet he must have seen. She ducked her head and more water splashed onto her dress but she didn't care. "I'm sorry, I don't know what to say."

"Neither do I; but maybe you would like to stay here a bit longer, and we can work this out together."

A pause; and then, "yes, I would like that. Thank you, Ethan."

———————————————

The sun dipped low, darkness spreading across the little neighbourhood despite it being only six o'clock in the evening. Through the living room window Claire watched the garden become bathed in the beautiful reds and yellows of sunset. She could have watched it for hours.

Then with a jolt she realised she had been out for *hours*. Her father was going to be *enraged*. With a gasp caught in her throat she whirled to Ethan, lips parted to voice her concern.

He was already on his feet, fetching her shawl as if he knew exactly what she needed. "You should go," he conceded, though his full lips pulled into a frown, "you need to talk to your family; especially your dad."

It was true; but the knowledge didn't make her feel any less concerned. She had ran from him, gone straight to Ethan - and Father was bound to know where she had gone. Even though all they had done was talk and eat dinner together, it was enough to be unforgivable in his eyes. What was she going to do?

Warmth settled across tense shoulders as Ethan draped the shawl around her. Claire smiled in thanks; but it was forced, false. The reality of the situation was settling in and it made her *ill*. She didn't want to imagine how Father was going to react.

"I know you said he wanted to disown you," Ethan muttered. He paused to think; or perhaps he was being careful of her boundaries. He was sweet - perhaps too much so. "I don't know him, but I have my own family. They say things they don't mean because they're angry or upset - or maybe *scared*. He might turn out to be more understanding than you think."

Claire hoped so. More than *anything,* she hoped so. "You don't know my father," she replied quietly. She didn't budge as Ethan settled on the arm of the sofa - but his closeness made her shift uncomfortably. Clearing her throat she continued, "I said a silly thing to prove a point and it turned him against me. Once he has set his mind on something it's impossible to change it."

Ethan shifted, and white teeth poked out as he chewed his lip in thought. It was a cute expression - one she wasn't used to. "What if we went to see him together?" Claire's eyes widened, coldness seeping into her skin - and Ethan quickly raised a hand in defeat. "Just listen to me. I know it sounds like an awful idea but... I don't know. Maybe if we both explained our side he would understand better. If he saw us together he might realise this is what you want."

Her cheeks flushed dark crimson and she ducked her head so he wouldn't see it spread across her face. This was all so new - so foreign - and frankly she didn't know what to do about it at all. A small laugh escaped her lips and she muffled it behind her palm. This was *absurd;* Ethan, her father, the entire thing. Like a bad dream she couldn't wake up from.

She had Ethan though, and whatever happened she knew he would stand by her.

"Come on Claire," he spoke softly, and then reached out to tug the shawl closer around her shoulders. "You can't put it off forever. Either you talk to him with me or alone, but it has to happen sometime."

He was right of course. Silently she nodded, her eyes flickering up to lock with his. They watched each other for one long moment, and Claire realised for the first time just how *handsome* he was. She had known from the moment she met him; but in the dim lighting of the room and the sunset behind him, he was stunning.

She shook her head as if to somehow dispel her thoughts, and when she jumped to her feet it was too quick, too skittish. EThan rose a brow in question but she said nothing to defend herself. Instead, "then I suppose we should go. I doubt your plan will work, but at this point I don't think I can make things worse." At least she sincerely *hoped* that was the case.

They left the house in silence, and when the cool air hit her face and rustled strands of dark hair poking free she said nothing. She hurried down the road with Ethan barely keeping up. She was equally desperate to get this over with and desperate to hide away and never see her father again.

"Slow down," Ethan murmured softly as he placed a hand against her slender shoulder. "Don't let your dad know he's rattled you like this."

He *had* 'rattled her' and Claire had to resist the urge to snap at him. Instead she took in a deep breath and forced her legs to slow. Although she still moved briskly, at least she wasn't leaving herself huffing for air.

Even so it took them barely ten minutes to reach her house. The path led them right to her doorstep and she stood, hands hovering over the wood without knocking. The energy had left her and she was just *tired*. Tired of fighting with her father and missing her mother and pretending as if her feelings for Ethan were just superficial. All she wanted was to be *herself.*

"Hey," Ethan whispered - and then he ghosted a kiss across her cheek. "You'll be fine."

That contact, so simple and barely there, lit up a fire in her cheeks and her stomach lurched into her chest. She couldn't help the grin that spread across her lips or the heavy relief that flooded through her veins. She didn't dare kiss back, but she reached out a small hand and clamped it around his.

Then with her free hand, she opened the front door and strode inside.

Susannah sat in the living room with a bundle of knitting on her lap. Her gaze drifted to Claire - and then widened as realisation settled in. When she saw Ethan, however, her expression soured. "Who is this?"

"Is someone here?" her father asked as he appeared at the top of the stairs. In the almost non-existent light he looked larger, more intimidating than ever. He descended the stairs with slow precision, eyes moving from Claire, then to Ethan, and back again. "Claire, who is this?" His voice echoed Susannah - but deeper, with a warning tone.

Claire swallowed but her words were stuck, her mind seizing up and suddenly it was as if she had no words at all.

Beside her, Ethan gave her hand a gentle squeeze. "My name's Ethan, sir. I came to try and-"

"Ethan?"

He stopped cold, and if he hadn't been holding Claire's hand she imagined Ethan would have stumbled back. His intake of breath was quiet but unmistakable as he moved closer to her, their arms brushing.

"Father *please,* we just came to explain ourselves. I just want you to *understand.*"

"Understand that you refuse to marry, yet you will be seen with *this* man? Understand that I told you not to come back to this home until you had agreed to my terms and yet *here you are?*" Her father stormed forward and this time both Ethan *and* Claire skittered back. "You never listen to a word I say. Both of you leave *now.*"

"Father, please don't do this-"

"You can't throw out your own daughter-"

"Wait!"

Claire's head spun, eyes snapping up to rest on Susannah. She stood in the living room doorway, eyes wide - and close to tears. She was taller than Claire - almost as tall as their father in fact - and when she stormed over she *demanded* attention. "You *cannot* tell her to leave. She's your daughter, my sister, and if you make her leave us then you really are a heartless man."

Claire flinched. No one spoke to him like that - not unless they *wanted* punishment. When Claire was ten years old she had spoken back to her father, called him a name. She had never dared do it again. Yet here Susannah was defending her, standing up to their father in a way she had *never* done before.

Her heart warmed, and for a moment she wondered if perhaps everything was going to be okay.

Her father was lost for words. His mouth opened and then closed as if he couldn't comprehend what Susannah had said. After a moment he seemed to gather his thoughts and said, "if she wants to be with this man I cannot stop her, but I won't allow her to live between two worlds. She must choose; her family, or *him.*"

Tears sprung to Claire's eyes and her mind whirled. He was demanding she *choose?* She was dizzy, her legs weak beneath her and for a moment she thought she might collapse; but Ethan's strong arms supported her and when he smiled, it lit up the entire room.

What he said next, however, made the world spin even more.

"What if I joined you? What if I learned about your way of life and maybe... maybe I could become Amish too."

"Ethan!" Claire gasped, spinning to face him and grabbing his shoulder so he spun too. "You can't. Our way of life is not like yours and- and you can't convert for me. You must be *genuine* and-"

"I *am* genuine. If it's the only way for us to be together, for you to live your life then *I'll do it.*" His eyes fixed on hers, caring and filled with warmth. No one had ever looked at her like this, with such love. Not since her mother had died and left her with a family that did not understand her.

A small huff left Susannah's lips as she regarded them. Though her lips curled in disgust her eyes showed understanding. "I might not like you, Ethan, but even I can't expect you to do this for my sister."

"I would. I haven't known her long, but I'd do anything for her."

Claire's heart *bloomed,* a smile spreading across her face so wide it *hurt.*

"Is it true? You would really do anything for Claire?"

She jumped at her father's voice, eyes snapping up to lock with his - but there was no anger there, not anymore. His expression was a mystery on a face usually so easy to read.

"Yes, I would."

The answer, so simple yet so *powerful,* left everyone in thick, tense silence. For a long moment it seemed as if no one wanted to be the first to speak; but it was her father who spoke first.

"I wouldn't ask that of you. Our way of life isn't easy; especially for someone who hasn't been brought up into it." He turned to Claire - and although his face was still unreadable, he gave a tiny smile. "The two of you mean a lot to each other, even I can see it. I won't lie to you and say I approve of it - but I cannot *stop you,* either."

"So you aren't angry?" Claire questioned in a wobbling voice.

"No. Not when I see you side by side, and now now that I know what this man is willing to do for you. The two of you remind me of what your mother and I used to be like."

Oh. *Oh.* Tears sprung to Claire's eyes once more and warm liquid rolled down her cheeks. "What now?"

"Now, you have to decide what you want to do. If Ethan is willing to join our way of life I will do everything I can to help; and if you wish to join *his,* then I will allow it too."

Speechless. She was utterly *speechless* despite the fact her mind was a whir of activity. She couldn't possibly focus on one thought for long enough to voice it. Instead she simply nodded, reaching out to squeeze her father's hand.

"We should leave you alone for a moment," Susannah whispered - and then both she and Father slipped from the hall, letting the living room door click closed between them.

Blinking away the tears Claire turned to Ethan - and then laughter burst from her without permission and without warning.

He joined, too - and then his lips caught hers in a brief, chaste kiss. He pulled back immediately as the laugh died on his lips and instead an apology tumbled forth. "Sorry, that was probably too forward of me, I didn't think-"

"Don't apologise," she interjected with a beaming smile, "though perhaps don't kiss me in my father's presence."

"Right. Obviously." He smiled sheepishly, eyes downcast. "So what do we do now?"

"Honestly," she confessed with a nervous shrug, "I don't know. All I *do* know is that while you're by my side, I'm willing to just see where things take us. Whatever happens, I know we can do it together."

Ethan beamed - and Claire knew she was *never* going to get fed up of that beautiful smile - and said "I agree."

AMISH SHADOWS

MONICA MARKS

40

Hannah leaned forward to pop the bread into the oven and raised herself to her full height, wiping her floured hands on her apron.

No sooner had she righted herself did she hear a crash from directly above her head.

She froze, momentarily unsure of if she had imagined it or not but a small voice in her head yelled at her to investigate.

Collecting herself quickly, she rushed from the kitchen and hurried up the unsteady stairs to the second floor.

They had needed repair for months, but it was only one more thing on the growing list which was not going to be done.

"*Daed*?" she called timidly as she approached his bedroom. "*Daed*, are you all right?"

There was no answer and Hannah felt her heart begin to hammer wildly in her chest.

She swallowed the lump in her throat and rapped on the faded wooden door.

"*Daed*?" she tried again, willing herself to be calm. "Daed, what happened?"

To her chagrin, there was still no reply and she eased the door open to peer inside the bedroom.

It was still a bright, warm May day but she would never have known it by the looks of her father's bed chambers.

Never mind the filthy clothes in arbitrary piles indifferently strewn over the floor and furniture alike, or the stench of stale, dirty air which hung over her.

The curtains, faded black without room for the most persistent ray of light, hung drawn and unmoving against a closed window.

Hannah felt herself growing dizzy with what she might find beneath the mound of covers tangled on the bed, but she tried to tell herself that she had been expecting something like this for years.

Still, she was not sure what she would do if she stumbled across her father's dead body laying on the mattress.

No amount of preparation could see her through such a horrific sight.

I have seen it before and I do not wish to ever see it again. Dear Gotte, please, not again.

"*Daed*?" she whispered. "Please speak to me..."

She cautiously approached the bed and closed her blue eyes, counting to five slowly before opening her eyes.

There was no one there.

Confused, she leaned in, touching the mass of blankets but her father was not in the middle of the mound.

"What are you doing in here?"

She whirled to confront the gruff voice behind her.

"*Daed*!" she exclaimed, exhaling in relief. "You are..."

She trailed off as she caught herself from saying what she was thinking.

"What was that crash?" she asked, quickly changing her tone into concern. "Are you all right?"

"I dropped the toilet lid," Joseph replied shortly, shuffling past her in a way that implied he was much older than his years.

Hannah caught a whiff of his sour scent and she wondered when was the last time he had bathed.

"I need to rest," Joe continued, reclaiming his spot on the mattress and turning his back to her. "Stop hovering."

Hannah stared at him for a long moment, a thousand different protests ready to spring from her lips but she clamped her lips together instead and turned away.

It wouldn't matter what she said, what argument she gave. No amount of cajoling or pleading would move her father from the darkness which had enveloped him since her mother had died six months earlier.

I do not know how much more of this I can take, Hannah thought but it was not the first time she had felt that way.

Bishop Schultz had assured her that time would heal Joe's pain and that *Gotte* and the community would guide them through such a trying experience, but Hannah no longer believed any of it.

At first, she had the utmost faith in everything the bishop had said.

"Your *Midder* passed away so unexpectedly," the kindly man had told her. "No one, least of all your father could have foreseen such a tragedy. To lose his wife in his own bed when she was barely forty years old is devastating, especially after the struggles your family has faced in the district."

Hannah nodded in agreement.

"An aneurysm is such a sudden way to go and accepting her death will take a great deal of healing. Your parents were married younger than most and they have overcome much together, as you know."

Hannah did not need to be reminded about the heartbreak her parents had endured. She had lived with it her entire life.

"Your *Midder* and *Vedder* had bond which was stronger than that of any other couple I know and now half of that is gone, without warning. Your *Vedder* must feel as if he has lost both his legs and his arms without her."

Hannah was certain that the bishop was right, but his words did not help her plight, especially when the days melted into weeks and the weeks, months of endless suffering.

The family and neighbors had been consistent about coming at the start.

Friends cooked and offered words of support, allowing Joe to grieve in peace but eventually their visits became less frequent and the alleviation they had provided in the beginning became one more chore for Hannah to work with when they failed to appear.

Then, just as suddenly, Maria stopped coming by to help tend the garden and chickens while Hannah maintained the shop and the neighbor's avoided discussing Joe as if he, too, had died.

Hannah knew that none of it was anyone responsibility but hers, yet she could not help but feel slightly resentful, especially of her older sister.

"Maria, you must stay until he is well. Everything is falling to pieces without him manning the store and dealing with customers," Hannah begged her sibling, but she could have anticipated the response as they entered the third month of their father's descent into despair. "The house – well, you can see what a state the house is in. Please, just come for a time and help me through."

Maria had shaken her dark red braid as if she had an answer already prepared.

"I have the new *boppli*," she protested. "I cannot just leave Aaron alone with the *kinder*. It is not fair to him."

"What about what is fair to *Daed*?" Hannah cried.

Or to me! She wanted to add but she dared not make it about herself.

Maria lowered her crystalline eyes.

"My duty is to my husband and *kinder* now, Hannah. You would understand if you were wed."

And how am I to wed if I am perpetually stuck caring for our parents? Hannah wanted to scream but she did not.

Like arguing with Joe, Maria would not be budged once her mind was made up.

For months, Hannah had been both working her father's general store, managing the accounts, ordering inventory and manning the small farm on which they lived but every day she felt more of herself slipping away.

Maria still did make an appearance every so often, but Hannah suspected that had more to do with alleviating her own guilt than it did with helping for when she left, Hannah would feel even more overwhelmed than before she had arrived.

"*Daed*," she called gently from the doorway as an afterthought. "Will you have something to eat today? I have just put fresh bread in the oven."

She waited for his customary refusal and he grunted as she had expected.

Sighing quietly, she closed the door to his room and resisted the urge to cry.

He would not eat and lay in bed, suffocating in his own filth.

For all Hannah knew, he was ill, but Joe would not permit a doctor to see him.

Occasionally, Hannah would wake during the wee hours of the morning and glimpse him sitting on one of the two rocking chairs on the porch, talking to her mother as if she was still alive.

He is spiralling into madness, Hannah thought, her heart breaking. *And I fear I am soon to join him.*

A pounding was pulsating in the back of Hannah's head, steady and rhythmic like the bass of a drum.

She was slowly growing aware of it but there was little she could do to stop it.

Her eyes were like leaden weights, glued together despite the struggle she put up to pry her lids apart.

Very slowly, she realized the incessant banging was not solely coming from her throbbing headache but from the front door.

She inhaled deeply and tried again to open her eyes.

They were nearly swollen shut and burning as she looked around her bedroom, gasping.

Full morning sunlight streamed through the dirty windows.

How long has it been since I've washed them? Hannah wondered, trying to collect herself and her thoughts.

It had to have been just after her mother had passed.

Has it really been a year since I've washed the windows?

Her mind did not seem to be registering reality but bit by bit, Hannah realized that not only had she slept in much later than she could justify, she was ill.

Each movement seemed excruciating as she managed to get herself off the bed and slip on a discarded work dress.

It was in dire need of a wash but that was less important than whomever seemed determined to knock down the front door.

Something must be terribly wrong, she thought, swallowing the sandpaper in her throat and stumbling down the hall toward the stairs.

Her father's door was closed as it always was, and Hannah felt a spark of annoyance course through her.

If the knocking had woken her from a fevered sleep, Joe had undoubtedly heard it too.

He cannot even be bothered to check and see what is the matter, she thought with some bitterness.

Her discontent had only mounted as Joe refused to accept help or rise from his depression.

Hannah was beginning to feel caged, uncertain and uncharacteristically angry.

Even Maria had stopped her weekly visits, citing Hannah's sour mood as her reasons.

"You seem to have this handled," Maria said smugly after Hannah had finally snapped one afternoon, two months earlier. "I see you do not need my help anymore."

"No," Hannah spat back. "I do not need your pretense of assistance, Maria. Go home and tend to your real family."

Hannah had regretted her harsh words, certainly after she realized how Maria's sporadic visits made a small difference, but she refused to ask her sister to return.

Everything was suffering but Hannah had no other recourse, not when there was nothing but Bishop Schultz's assurances that things would improve.

She stopped attending worship because she feared she would lash out at the well-meaning man, but it seemed her mood was following her father's into a disheartened abyss.

"*Mein Gotte*!" Hannah snapped as she threw open the door. "What is going on?"

She was taken aback to see an Englischer standing before her on the porch, a frown on his creased face.

A light snow was falling over the lawn, covering the old but Hannah barely noticed the flakes dancing against the surprisingly bright sunlight.

"I am sorry to disturb you, ma'am. Is Joseph Gerig home?"

Hannah's pulse began to race slightly, and she felt a sweat break out over her forehead.

"No," she fibbed quickly, envisioning her father drowning beneath the unwashed sheets in his bedroom. "May I help you?"

He smiled tightly and without mirth.

Hannah felt herself swoon slightly and she could not say if it was due to her fever or the sense of impending dread growing in her gut.

"I am afraid this is something I must speak with Mr. Gerig about," he insisted, handing her a card. "Will you please have him visit Harrison Savings and Loans in Millersburg immediately. It is a matter of great urgency."

Hannah accepted the card and looked down at the name, her heart in her throat.

Nathan Keller, Mortgage Specialist.

Hannah closed her clear blue eyes and allowed herself to fall against the frame of the door.

"This is about the store mortgage, isn't it?" she sighed, biting on her lower lip.

"I'm sorry, ma'am but I'm not at liberty to discuss this matter with anyone but the mortgage holder. Please ensure that he does receive the message."

"I will," Hannah sighed, feeling the little bit of color left in her face drain away.

"What is your name, ma'am? I want to make sure I have it on record that I did speak to someone before any actions were taken."

Oh Gotte, please, not now, she prayed silently. *We can't lose the store. How will we live?*

"Hannah Gerig. I am his daughter."

Nathan Keller nodded stiffly.

"Have a nice day, Ms. Gerig," he said flatly, turning toward a car parked just up the road.

She slowly shut the door and leaned up against it, tears burning beneath her lids, but she refused to let them fall.

I have already lost my mother, father and sister, Hannah thought firmly. *I will not lose my home too!*

Before she could reconsider what she was doing, Hannah took the stairs, two at a time, her dress almost tripping her at the hem, but she barely noticed it.

In a haze, she threw open the door to her father's bedroom, the brass handle hitting the wall with a bang.

Joe flipped around to stare at her with bleary eyes.

"Hannah, what in *Gotte's* name – "

"Get up!" she rasped, her voice choked with emotion and sickness. "Get up right this instant!"

He gaped at her.

"What has gotten into you, *dochder*? Are you ill? Get out and leave me be!"

"No!" Hannah howled. "I will not! I will not!"

Without warning, she burst into tears, crumbling to her knees on the floor and buried her pale face in her hands.

"Hannah! What has happened?" Joe demanded but she could not look up. She was defeated, her soul felt crushed.

For over a year she had tried her best to hold the remnants of her family together, but she could do it no longer. She did not have the strength.

I just want to die, I want to waste away just like Daed is doing. They can carry us out of the house together when they repossess it.

"Hanny?"

Unexpectedly, she felt a cool hand on her shoulder and she managed to peer up at her father's concerned face.

"You are feverish!" he gasped. "Hannah, you must get to bed right away."

She shook her head.

She could not move. She wanted to lay on his floor and let it swallow her, but Joe pulled on her arm until she finally obliged.

"Why are you so upset?" he murmured as he perched on the side of her bed, touching her face with worry. "Are you delirious?"

She moaned slightly and shook her head.

"No, *Daed*," she sobbed. "The bank was here. We are going to lose everything. I failed us. We are done."

"Shh," he cooed, brushing her messy red strands away from her translucent skin. "That is nonsense. We are not going to lose anything, Hannah. I will tend to this, I promise. You have nothing to worry about but becoming well."

She scoffed.

"And who will tend to you?" she choked, her headache growing worse.

His hand cupped around her face.

"Look at me, *liebchen*," he said quietly, and her heart swelled at the sound of an endearment she had not heard in too long.

Reluctantly, she peered into his face.

"I will tend to me," he replied quietly. "You have carried us on your shoulders for far too long. It is I who has failed you and I am sorry. Things will change now. I swear it, Hannah."

She began to bawl then, hot tears flowing down her cheeks in streams, but Hannah knew that for once she was not crying from misery.

She was sobbing with relief.

As promised, things did change in the Gerig household, but Hannah was not sure if they were better or worse.

While Joe no longer lay in his bed, wasting away day after day, he was not the same loving man he had been before her mother had passed.

There was a certain relief to sharing the chores again, but Joe seemed to be more of a machine than a man and while he went about his days as he had in the past, Hannah could not help but feel as if he was gone.

"It is wonderful to see your *Vedder* working again," Bishop Schultz told her one afternoon when they had chanced upon each other in Millersburg. "I told you he would eventually overcome his sadness, did I not?"

Hannah refrained from telling the bishop what she thought of his advice.

If I had not almost given up myself, he would have remained in that state forever, she thought with bitterness. *And even now, he is not here.*

It had been eight months since they had almost lost the business but to Hannah, it felt like it had been a decade.

The feeling of stagnation had not disappeared but suddenly Hannah did not know what to do to make it better.

She had always believed that once Joe picked himself out of bed, he would be fine, but she was wrong.

He was like a walking corpse, acting but not feeling as if any emotion he had once possessed had died with his wife.

She said none of her true thoughts and instead smiled weakly.

"Yes, Bishop," she replied.

"I expect that I will see you both at service on Sunday?" he asked, and Hannah lowered her eyes, not wanting to lie to him.

"I will be there," she said slowly.

"And Joe?"

Hannah shrugged her slender shoulders slightly.

"I cannot speak to his plans," she answered quietly but she already knew her father would not attend worship.

When she tried to speak to him about it, he seemed to shut down even more and Hannah did not know what more to do.

Bishop Schultz narrowed his brown eyes.

"I think it is high time I paid Joe a visit," he muttered, his brow furrowing in disappointment.

Hannah raised her shoulders again.

"If you believe it will help, Bishop," she sighed but she had little faith in the man's ability to bring her father out of the darkness.

Still, it would be a relief to have someone else try.

Maria had almost stopped coming by the farm altogether and while Hannah would see her at worship, her sister rarely asked about their father as if the matter was resolved.

Hannah had never felt so alone.

When she arrived home that afternoon, her father was already back from the store.

"*Daed*?" she called, concern flooding her chest. "Why are you home so early?"

She cautiously walked up the steps, staring at his face for any signs of trouble.

It was unbearably hot, even for early July but Joe seemed almost content as he rocked slowly in his rocker, his straw hat pulled square over his blue eyes.

Yet Hannah was sure there was a smile on his face.

She gasped, trying to remember the last time she had seen his lips curl in such a way.

He didn't seem to notice her at first and Hannah's heart raced as she gently sat in the rocking chair her mother had once claimed as her won, facing her father.

"*Daed*?" she whispered, a part of her wanting to relish the almost serene expression on his face but she needed to know why he was happy.

As if she had yelled in his ear, his usual crestfallen expression recaptured his face and he turned to look at her with almost surprised blue eyes.

"Oh," he said. "You've returned. "

She nodded slowly.

"What are you doing home so early? Did something happen at the shop?"

He shook his head.

"No," he replied quickly, rising from the rocker but not before Hannah caught his cheek stain slightly rose. "I have them polishing the floors this afternoon."

Hannah's brow furrowed.

"They could not come later in the day?" she asked, confused. Typically, it was not a chore he would have ordered during work hours.

"It is the only time they had available!" he snapped defensively.

Hannah felt herself growing more confused.

They had been using the same cleaning company for years. It seemed unlikely that they would not make the time, regardless of their schedule.

"I will have a talk with Mr. Parsons," she said, rising to follow him back into the house. "That is unacceptable."

To her shock, he spun, glaring.

"You will not question me!" he shouted, and Hannah was sure she had never seen his face so red.

He didn't give her an opportunity to respond, tossing his hat aside and retreating to the kitchen as Hannah gaped after him.

What in Gotte's name was that about? She wondered, leaning down to retrieve his discarded hat but she could not understand.

Is he falling again?

Joe's behavior became more suspect as the weeks passed, and Hannah was consumed with the helpless feeling that she had been there before.

He acts so secretive, but he seems happier...at least until he senses me nearby and he loses his private smile. Is he unraveling again?

She grew more concerned but there was no cause for it.

Each day, he seemed to retreat into himself more, but it was not the same as it had been after her mother had passed. There did not appear to be a cloud hanging over him.

Joe still did not attend church services every second Sunday and on the day they were scheduled to host worship, he disappeared, leaving Hannah to organize the event alone.

"Where is Daed?" Maria demanded, aghast that he was not present.

Hannah cast her sister a look of annoyance.

"I have no idea," she replied.

"People are talking that he is not here," Maria moaned. "I am humiliated!"

Hannah felt herself stiffen as she peered at her sister through her peripheral vision.

"What have you to be embarrassed about?" she asked shortly. "People barely remember you are part of this family."

Shocked, Maria spun and gaped at her.

"What is that supposed to mean?" she demanded.

"Nothing," Hannah muttered, turning away to join the district in the yard.

"I have done everything I can – "

"Oh just stop!" Hannah snapped. "I am in no mood to listen to your self-pity, Maria. Please, go be with your husband and children. I have work to do."

As she stepped into the blazing sunlight, Amelia Fisher touched her arm and peered at her with concern.

"How are you, Hanny?" she asked.

Hannah studied her warily, knowing that Amelia would not have sought her out to be friendly.

"I am well. Yourself?"

Amelia nodded gravely.

"I only ask because, well, I am worried about Joe," Amelia continued, and Hannah resisted the urge to scream.

"*Daed* is doing very well," she lied. "But I will pass along your sentiments."

Amelia's green eyes grew wide.

"I imagine he is with...well, you know," she continued as Hannah tried to pass by.

Hannah froze.

"I have no idea where my *Vedder* is today," she retorted, gritting her teeth. "And I must lay the bread on the table. Everyone is about to eat, Amelia."

"Oh, of course," Amelia said but she did not step aside. "It must be very uncomfortable. I did not mean to embarrass you."

Hannah stared at her with cold blue eyes.

"I have no idea what you're talking about," she said flatly. "I have no reason to be embarrassed. It is *Daed's* choice whether he chooses to worship and – "

Amelia gasped, her hand flying to her mouth.

"Oh, no!" she cried with faux surprise. "You do not know!"

"Know what?" Hannah almost yelled. "What trouble are you stirring up now, Amelia?"

The brunette turned red with anger.

"I do not stir up trouble," she bit back. "And if my widowed *Vedder* was courting an Englischer I would want someone to tell me!"

A wave of dizziness flooded Hannah and her eyes became slits.

"What lies are you spreading?" Hannah hissed. "How dare you!"

Amelia sneered slightly but shrugged her shoulders.

"You can believe what you wish but everyone knows he has been spending time with the new school teacher from Millersburg Elementary. If you weren't hiding here all the time, you would know it too!"

Amelia stormed away, and Hannah's heart was about to leap from her chest.

Daed would not be courting anyone and certainly not an Englischer, she thought firmly but the more she considered Amelia's words, the more her heart sank.

Suddenly, her father's behavior made much more sense.

Oh Daed, she thought mournfully. *What are you doing?*

She loathed what she was doing but she had been left with little choice.

Ducking down behind his cart, Hannah poked her head out around the side of the wagon and watched as her father closed the store, glancing about furtively before starting down North Jackson Street.

It was far too early to close the shop but that was the least of Hannah's concerns as she followed from a safe distance.

He turned onto North Clay and then again on East Clinton where he finally stopped before an old Victorian house, trimmed in wood lace.

Hannah remained hidden behind a tree and watched as a middle-aged woman came out to greet him and Joe smiled broadly.

She was certainly an Englischer and even from the distance between them, Hannah could see the glint of her green eyes as they sparkled in the sunlight.

Her body language suggested that she was comfortable with Joe and Hannah could see he felt the same.

Her heart seemed to stop beating as the two sat on the steps of the house, talking.

Of course, she was too far away to hear the words, but it was obvious that they were enjoying one another's company.

Hannah slumped against the solid oak, a slew of emotions coursing through her.

She lost track of time as she studied their interaction but when she had seen enough, she slowly turned and made her way back toward the district.

The weight of the past two years was bearing down on her shoulders as she walked, a jumble of thoughts coursing through her as she tried to make sense of what she had learned.

As if in a fog, she recalled the six months her father had spent laying in bed, withering away while she fought to keep going.

She remembered the pitying looks of the community when he did not appear to worship and the unsolicited advice of Bishop Schultz who believed he was helping.

How much have I endured because I have waited for Daed to overcome his grief, to be the man he was before Mammi died? And now he has found an Englischer and continues to retreat into himself.

Hannah could imagine what Maria would say when she learned about the school teacher.

Hannah needed find a way to make things right again and she knew hard choices were on the horizon.

It was not until she had reached home that she determined what she was going to do.

The lamps were out when he arrived home and for a fleeting moment, Joe exhaled with relief.

Hannah is asleep, he thought, climbing the steps of the porch but his sense of calm was short lived when he saw a shadow in Elizabeth's rocking chair.

Joe gasped in shock.

"Hannah!" he cried, startled. "What are you doing sitting in the dark, *liebchen*?"

"Come and sit with me, *Daed*," Hannah said quietly, and Joe felt a shiver of apprehension slither through his body.

"I am very tired, Hanny," he told her. "I have had a long day at the store."

Even in the pale light of the moon, he saw a small, sardonic smile form on her lips.

"What is her name, *Daed*?" she asked, her tone so low, he barely heard the words.

Joe swallowed quickly.

"I do not know what you're talking about, Hannah. I must sleep."

"I have been sitting here, rocking back and forth for hours," she told him as if he was not about to walk away. "I know now why you felt like you could talk to Mammi on those nights when you came out here."

Joe paused, his pulse quickening.

"You saw me?" he asked gruffly.

"I did," she replied. "And as I sit here, I feel like she is here with me. Come and sit for a moment, Daed."

Joe shook his head, guilt sweeping through his body.

"Hannah, another night."

"How old were you when you and *Mammi* married?" she asked.

Joe scowled but he was grateful that the darkness hid his blush of defiance.

"What kind of question is that?" he demanded. "You know we married when we were seventeen."

"You were so young," she sighed.

"Hannah, what is this about?" he growled but he suspected he knew.

"What do you think made your marriage successful?"

"I am tired!"

His tone was much harsher than he intended but Hannah did not seem to hear him as she continued.

"You and *Mammi* endured so much together. You buried a son. You lost a business and almost lost this house several times."

"Hannah, I do not know what you think you know – "

"What is her name, *Daed*?"

Joe gulped back the lump in his throat, memories of his late wife flittering through his mind.

I was such a fool to think I could hide this from Hannah.

"Shari," he whispered. "Shari Chisholm."

Hannah nodded.

"She has kind eyes."

Joe tensed.

"She is a friend."

"Is she?"

Hannah rose and approached him, biting on her lower lip.

"You and *Mammi* had a difficult life together. When she died, you must have felt as if a part of you died too."

"I did," he muttered. "I still do."

"But I think about how you and she managed to overcome it all and still raise us and build your business. Many others would have given up."

"We had you and Maria to keep us going," he replied, staring into his daughter's eyes.

"And you had each other," she finished. "That is how you managed. That is why you fell apart when she died."

Joe studied her face, shame in his eyes.

"I will not pursue Shari anymore," he breathed. "I see the error of my ways, Hanny. Forgive me for upsetting you."

A perplexed look crossed over Hannah's face.

"What error, *Daed*? You have done nothing wrong. That is what I am trying to say."

They eyed each other but Joe was confused.

"Wh- I do not understand."

"You need a partner, someone to depend upon when life grows difficult. When *Mammi* died, you lost that, but I saw you today with Shari and it was the first time I have seen you smile in years."

Joe frowned.

"That is not true, *liebchen*. You make me smile..." he trailed off as Hannah shook her head.

"No, *Daed*. I do not."

Joe sighed heavily, tears burning under his eyes.

"I have lost my way," he choked, sinking into his rocking chair. "I feel like I have been drowning I do not know how to swim to the surface of the lake and catch my breath."

He inhaled sharply.

"I have never loved another woman in this way besides your *Midde*r."

"I can see that. It shines through in the way you look at her."

"I should not have allowed for this to happen. I am conflicted, and I do not know how to overcome my guilt but the feelings I have for Shari are so strong. I cannot deny them and yet..."

"Shari will help you through this, *Daed*," Hannah said confidently. "You must allow her to do that."

Joe grimaced slightly.

"For what?" he sighed. "There can be no future between us."

"Why not?"

Joe looked up sharply.

"Because she is *Englisch* and I am Amish, of course. You are being coy."

"Am I?" Hannah replied. "I thought I was being honest. Possibly more honest than you."

"Mind your tongue, *dochder*. I am still your *Vedder* and I will not tolerate insolence."

"I do not mean to sound insolent. I mean for you to open your eyes and look at things clearly for once."

Joe scoffed.

"And what do you propose, Hanny? That I continue our relationship in private? It is not fair to Shari."

"That is not fair to anyone," Hannah agreed. "I do not think you should hide at all."

He laughed mirthlessly but Hannah was not finished.

"You have not been to worship in how long? You have had one foot off the land since *Mammi* died. If things should progress between you and Shari, you will deal with it accordingly."

"And then what? Imagine the embarrassment it will cause you and your sister."

Hannah reached for her father's hand and squeezed it tightly.

"All I have hoped for since *Mammi* passed is for you to be the man you were before. And today was the first time I have seen a trace of that man. If you believe that I would trade that because of the talk of some gossips, you are mistaken, *Daed*."

She gazed at him and Joe was overcome by the emotion in her face.

"You are wrong, Hanny," he told her, returning her warm touch with vigor. "It is not Shari who has helped me get through this. Without you, I would be a pile of bones in a dirty bed right now."

She smiled.

"I will always be at your side, *Daed*," she promised, and Joe sobbed, lowering his eyes as the truth of her words filled his heart.

He wiped the corner of his eye and nodded his head.

"I am truly blessed," he replied and for the first time since Elizabeth had passed, he genuinely felt it was so.

"*Daed*, I wish you would have had her come to the house," Hannah whispered as they stood on the stoop of the Victorian house where Shari lived.

She would have liked to wipe her hands on her dress, but she held a plate of freshly baked cookies in her hands.

"She insisted on meeting you here," Joe replied. "She claims she has a surprise for you."

Before Hannah could question him, the door swung inward.

Shari Chisolm smiled at them and Hannah could see that she had been right about the woman's sparkling eyes.

"Welcome!" Shari cried, leaning forward to embrace Hannah.

"Oh!" Hannah gasped at the unexpected gesture, but she laughed and allowed her father's girlfriend to hug her.

Instantly, she relaxed under the woman's touch.

"I have been so forward to meeting you, Hannah!" Shari exclaimed, ushering them inside. "Your dad goes on and on about you, but he never did tell me just how beautiful you are!"

A slow flush crept up Hannah's face as they entered the living room.

Hannah opened her mouth to thank her, but the words froze on her lips.

Inside, a tall man stood, his back to them as he peered out the window but even without seeing his face, Hannah could see he was well built.

He turned slightly, and Hannah's breath caught in her throat.

"Hello," he said, placing his drink on the window sill. He extended his palm, a wide smile gracing his even, angular features.

"Hello," Hannah breathed, unable to steady her heart as she stared into his eyes.

"Jamie, this is my beau, Joe Gerig and his lovely daughter, Hannah. Joe and Hannah, this is my second cousin, Jamie Chisholm."

Hannah almost pushed her father aside to accept his outstretched hand and she seemed to lose herself in his gaze.

"Hello," she said again, and she wished she could bring herself to say something else, but no other words seemed to come to mind.

"Hello," Jamie replied, his grin widening. It was as if Shari and her father had suddenly disappeared from the room.

"What did I tell you?" she heard Shari chuckle behind her. "I am a natural matchmaker."

The words should have given Hannah a spark of embarrassment, but it did not.

Instead, she felt as if a hundred bricks had been lifted from her body.

Daed is fine, finally. He is happy, and I am free to move forward with my life.

The realization filled her with an elation so strong, she was almost knocked down.

Reluctantly, she turned her head and glanced at Joe over her shoulder.

He smiled at her tenderly and Hannah knew that it was okay to breathe again.

AMISH INDIANA

'Two are better than one; because they have a good reward for their labor. For if they fall, the one will lift up his fellow: but woe to him that is alone when he falleth; for he hath not another to help him up.'
- Ecclesiastes 4:9-10

It was a beautiful summer day in Nappanee, Indiana. The sun was shining brightly down upon the grassy fields, illuminating the deep red paint of the detached wooden houses in which Kayla Albrecht's family and friends all lived. There was not even a singular cloud in the air above her and the cerulean blanket of sky stretched out for miles and miles before disappearing beyond the distant horizon. A gentle wind caused the crops to sway and bend as though moving to an inaudible rhythm just out of Rebecca's reach. Butterflies danced together, fluttering their wings in the breeze. All around her, the miracle of God's gift of life was wonderful and plain to see except for in the one place Kayla wanted it to be the most—the eyes of her best friend.

It was early in the morning, but that mattered not to most of the townsfolk. Mr. Fisher was already strolling past her on his way to plow the fields and Mrs. Sutter was dressed in her usual blue day dress and white bonnet as she sat on the verdant grass and recited prayers to her two youngest in a sweet, melodious voice. The smell of freshly baked bread was wafting out of her own house behind her as her younger sister began her daily chores. Kayla was envious of them and how quickly they could forget. After all, her best friend had only been buried a few days prior. She wondered if her agony might ever cease or whether she would dwell in this grief forever. It seemed she had little time to contemplate this we sue was forced out of her reverie by a familiar and welcome face.

"Mornin', Kayla," a deep, cheery voice greeted.

"Stephen," she muttered, caught a little off guard and wondering how he had snuck up on her in such a short period of time. "Shouldn't you be tending to the crops by now?"

The handsome and young man in front of her smiled and tipped his hat toward her. "You caught me, Kayla. There ain't never getting anything past you, is there?" His joyful demeanor only served to highlight the young woman's own bitterness and she scowled.

"Quit your games, Stephen, and just get to the point, would you?" Kayla snapped.

He sighed and scrubbed a hand through his light brown beard with smatterings of ginger. His light blue eyes were kind as they looked down into hers with the same expression he had been giving her all week—pity. Kayla knew her boyfriend meant well. She knew that he tried to understand what she was going through, but he simply couldn't. No one could.

"I asked Mr. Graber to start a little later today," Stephen began to explain as he adjusted his straw hat. "I thought we could spend a little time together. Maybe go for a walk?"

Kayla knew he was trying, but this certainly wasn't what she needed right now. He hadn't even considered her plans. He just assumed she could drop everything on a whim because he wanted her to. She let out a sigh and tucked a stray lock of her brunette hair that she could never quite tame behind her ear for the third time that morning.

"You might have time to waste, Stephen, but I don't," she told him curtly and brushed past him to continue walking around to her family's back garden. "I have chores to complete still. I need to hang the laundry out to dry and then I'm not quite sure whether Elizabeth has time today to churn the butter, so that'll be my next job and then after that, I promised myself I'd go see Jacob—"

"You're seeing Jacob again?" Stephen interrupted with a scoff. "Look, I think it's a noble thing you're doing for him and all. I'm glad he has someone like you to deliver food and tidy the house up a little for him. I want to be supportive and I've tried really hard the last few weeks, but now I'm worried. You're spending more time with him lately than your own boyfriend. It's really making me start to wonder if—"

"If what?" Kayla spat, dropping the basket of wet clothing in his arms onto the grass and stomping her feet as she whirled and closed the distance between them. Her emerald eyes blazed bright with rage. "My best friend *died*, Stephen. Just a few weeks ago. Do you remember that? You should do. Lauren was a big part of this village. You grew up with her just like you grew up with me and yet, it doesn't seem like you care. Instead, you're getting jealous because I'm trying to help her *grieving husband*. A widower who has a baby to take care of."

After her tirade, Kayla stopped for a sharp intake of breath. Her gaze dropped down to the floor and away from the man whom up until recently had been her rock and her future. Now, Kayla wasn't sure what he was anymore. She shook her head as tears began to form in her eyes and she turned away to retrieve her basket.

"May God forgive your jealousy, I'm not sure I can."

With that, Kayla continued on her path and left her boyfriend to stare dumbstruck in the dust behind her.

***

After her morning chores, Kayla found the time to freshen up and change her clothes into a pale-yellow linen dress with a white cloth bonnet which had a little yellow trim. Her mother had made it for her three years ago on her eighteenth birthday and Kayla treasured it with all her heart. So, she brushed down the skirt to clear it of any dirt and debris before she knocked on the house of the Rabers. She held a basket full of bread, a pie, and a block of cheese in the crook of her elbow and plastered a kind on her face. In spite of her own sour mood, it was important that Kayla didn't bring Jacob down with her. After all, he was going through much worse than she was.

The door swung open and revealed a disheveled Jacob. His eyes were red-rimmed and decorated with red rivets running along the whites. Underneath, the skin was purpling and it was wholly distracting from the pretty blue eyes he had that many girls had admired him for in his youth. He was dressed, but his shirt remained untucked, his waistcoat was unbuttoned, and his blond beard untrimmed. It was clear that this was a man who was struggling.

There was no straw hat atop his head and Kayla could see the messy mop of blond hair sat there, unbrushed and untamed. She offered him a sympathetic smile and sighed. "Good morning, Jacob," she greeted in a gentle voice. "I brought you and Adam some food. May I come in?"

He grunted in response and nodded before turning away from the doorway and chasing after the high-pitched cries of a young child. Kayla let herself into the abode and firmly shut the door behind her. The house appeared just as she had left it the day before: simple, a little messy, and sparsely decorated. She followed the sounds of Adam's cries to the living room and admired the plain decoration there. With merely a sofa, a couple of armchairs, a coffee table, a few bookshelves lining the walls, and Adam's bassinet, it was clear that Jacob was a forthright and modest man.

Though his skill in woodworking was evident, there was another task that Jacob Raber struggled with and Kayla had seen it first-hand ever since Lauren had died. No matter how much he cooed and cuddled and comforted, Jacob couldn't seem to quell the cries of his child. It was as though the child himself was also in mourning for a mother he had barely known.

As Jacob leaned over the Moses basket and tried to calm the child, Kayla looked on with difficulty. She hadn't wanted to interfere too much in Jacob's life since his wife's death. She hadn't known him very well outside of her friendship with Lauren as he'd only moved to the town a few months before they were wed. He was a private fellow and oftentimes kept to himself, but Lauren had told Kayla many a wonderful thing about him. Now, however, Kayla couldn't help but intervene. Her compassionate nature preventing her from being able to leave two humans clearly in dire need of aid.

"I could help you, you know," she mentioned with a cough. Kayla shifted from one foot to the other a little awkwardly. "With the baby, I mean."

The young Amish man before her turned to look at her strangely, his head tilted to the side a little. "You really want to help me?" he asked in a quiet voice.

"O-of course!" she exclaimed, a little caught off guard. "That's what we do in this community, right? We're a family."

"Yeah, I suppose," Jacob agreed with a nod. "No one else has offered, though."

"Well, they probably will," Kayla replied with a slight shrug before reaching up and tucking her hair behind her ear once more as it sprung out and blocked her vision. "Would you like some help, Jacob?"

An expression Kayla didn't understand flickered over her neighbor's face before he smiled widely at her for the first time since Lauren died. "Yes. Yes, please, that would be wonderful." He strode across the room and embraced her tight. His arms were fierce and strong around her. Kayla felt him clinging to her as though she were the only raft in a tumultuous ocean.

Gingerly, she lifted her arms and pat his back in what she hoped was a comforting manner. "Then, let me take little Adam for you today, okay?" she whispered, her pats now turning into rubs as she tried to soothe him. "I'll feed him, take care of him, and we'll go out for a stroll in the nice warm sunshine. It's important that he gets to see the beauty and wonders of God's green Earth all around us, even when he's just a baby."

Finally, Jacob pulled away and swiped at his wet eyes. "That would be great, thank you, Kayla. It'll give me a chance to tidy the house a little bit and myself." He let out a little chuckle and swiped a hand through the mop on his head. "Are you sure you're okay looking after him?" he queried as an afterthought. "You don't have children, do you?"

Kayla smiled back at him and placed a gentle hand on his arm. "I will be absolutely fine, Jacob," she assured him. "I don't have children myself, but I've helped out with my younger siblings ever since Mother died and I used to help Lauren with Adam all the time. You have nothing to worry about."

Though Kayla had intended to be comforting, the mention of Lauren's name only seemed to serve Jacob as a reminder of what he had lost. Fresh tears pricked behind his eyes, threatening to fall and she heard him gulp audibly.

"Yes, yes, okay," he agreed with a shaky nod of his head. "You can see yourself out, right?" With that, Jacob swept out of the room and Kayla heard his loud footsteps on the creaky stairs. She let out a sigh and rubbed a hand over her face. She hoped she hadn't said anything wrong. It was such a difficult time for everyone and she didn't want to add to it.

Now, however, her focus would be on the tiny bundle of joy crying from his crib. She stepped forward and smiled down on little Adam who was bundled in a blanket. She shushed him and lifted him from the basket before rocking him slowly from side to side. Within no time at all, she had managed to quiet the cranky baby and proceeded to collect some milk for him.

Once he had been fed, Kayla went back to the entryway of the house and lay Adam down in the rich oak baby carriage. There was a plush, cushioned lining inside that he immediately sunk into comfortably. Kayla set up the parasol above him to keep the sun from hurting his young eyes and then made for the doorway.

As she pushed the young boy out of his house, Kayla caught sight of someone she hadn't been expecting to see: Stephen. He was stood at the entrance gate to the Raber's garden and looked at her grimly. She really didn't have time to deal with more of his petty nonsense today, especially not if she was going to devote her time and attention to the poor baby.

So, Kayla pushed down the pebbled path and as she reached her boyfriend, she asked, "Are you following me now?"

Stephen let out a huff and shook his head. "I wanted to apologize, Kayla," he began with a sigh. "I was way out of line this morning and I'm so sorry. I want you to know, I didn't mean it. I just miss you is all."

Kayla listened intently and then nodded. "I understand, but Stephen I really am just helping Jacob out in Lauren's stead. Surely, you must have a little compassion for a young man who has lost the love of his life?"

"Of course, I do, Kay," he told her in earnest. "My head was just a little muddled is all. I hope you can forgive me."

"Of course, Stephen." She smiled at him and then glanced down at little Adam in the carriage. "I must get going now if we are to soak up as much of this summer sun as is possible. Isn't that right, little one?" Her last question was directed at the cute baby who was squirming happily and sucking on his thumb.

"I'll see you later?" Stephen asked in a hopeful voice, his eyes wide and innocent.

"See you later, Stephen."

Once Kayla had said her goodbyes, she set off in the direction of the wheat fields where her and Lauren used to play as children. She began to recite stories of herself and Lauren growing up to Adam. She hoped that somewhere inside he might understand her words and it might comfort him during this period of grief. She hoped Adam could understand that one day he would be reunited with his mother in the Kingdom of Heaven and that she would be smiling down upon them now. Perhaps Lauren was the cause of the sunny weather. Her brilliant smile at the sight of her baby causing the friendly, bright rays of light which warmed her skin.

Please, God, look after Lauren and my mother until I may rejoin them in Heaven.

***

Six months had passed and Kayla had a new daily routine. Every day, she would complete her morning chores as quickly as possible and then head on over to the Raber's residence where she would have a pleasant lunch with Jacob and Adam before taking the littlest one out for a stroll along the town. When the weather was terrible, however, Kayla had no choice but to entertain Adam inside the house while Jacob continued with his own chores, work, and maintaining the house. As such, the two had spent far more time together than Kayla had imagined she ever would and strange feelings had begun to stir within her. Perhaps it was their proximity or the domesticity of the two of them looking after a child together, but she had begun to see why Lauren had been so attracted to Jacob in the first place.

Now that he'd had more time to mourn and move on, Jacob had begun to look like his old self once again. His beard was neatly trimmed, his hair was washed and brushed daily, and his clothes always looked clean and pristine. Kayla found herself able to look past the grieving widower she had come to know the last few months to see the funny, kind, and hard-working side of Jacob.

That day when she turned up at Jacob's house, she had done so with a parasol in hand. The rain outside was unrelenting and even the short walk down the road had been enough for the bottom of her day dress and her shoes to be completely soaked. Kayla let herself into the house as had become their custom. She shook her dress out as much as she could onto the porch before toeing her shoes off and leaving them upside down to dry near the entrance of the house.

"Jacob?" she called out when she finally entered and closed the door behind her. It was eerily quiet in the house and for a moment,

Kayla wondered if they had left the house. That was absurd, however, since the weather would hardly permit it for Jacob, let alone the baby!

"Jacob?" she called out once more as she left her parasol at the door and shrugged off her shawl from her shoulder. She crept further through the house until she reached the dining room and her jaw dropped.

"I thought you might want something warm after your walk here," Jacob told her with a kind smile. "Given the unpleasant weather outside." He gestured to the table where a hot teapot sat alongside two empty cups on top of saucers. Steam was rising from the pot and Kayla could already feel the warmth of the liquid soothing her cold body. Next to it was also a fresh cake and a pie. Kayla eyed it suspiciously.

"You baked a pie and a cake?" she queried. That was certainly not Jacob's usual forte.

"Oh, heavens no," he rushed to assure her with a chuckle. "Mrs. Sutter owed me a favor."

"You're too kind," Kayla told him and sat down to tuck into the wonderful treats laid out before her. A thrum of pleasure ran through her at the thought that Jacob had orchestrated this on her behalf. *Has he been thinking of me often outside of our routine?* she wondered and found that it caused a warmth to rush through her that had nothing to do with the tea in her cup.

***

When the leaves began to change to their tawny colors and drift along the breeze, Kayla had grown accustomed to her lone walks with Adam and enjoyed using them as a time to help him learn about his mother, God, and the importance of the life they lived here in Napanee. So, when Kayla arrived one pleasantly warm morning and began to get Adam settled in his carriage, she was surprised to see Jacob also pulling on his jacket and boots.

"Do you have somewhere to be, Jacob?" she asked curiously, one eyebrow quirked in confusion.

"No," he replied simply with a knowing smile as he grabbed his straw hat and placed it on top of his head. "I just fancied a walk is all."

"You're coming with us?"

Jacob paused for a moment as he contemplated Kayla's reaction. "Would you not like me to?"

"Well..." Kayla considered the question for a second before realizing that she was being foolish. "It was just a surprise, I'm sorry. Of course, you can come."

Jacob nodded and buttoned up his coat before crossing the room and opening the front door. "Ladies first," he told her with a grin.

Kayla smiled back and pushed the carriage out onto the porch. She took a deep breath in and enjoyed the fresh, pine air which surrounded them. She tightened her grip on the carriage in front of her to calm her nerves at the change in plans as she told herself over and over again, *Everything is fine, Kayla. You do not need to be nervous about spending time with Jacob. There is nothing romantic between you two. He is merely a friend who needs your help, that is all.*

Before she had even realized, they had reached the fields just beyond the residential section of the town and the clouds had begun to disperse enough that the sun shone a little brighter down upon the trio. Kayla closed her eyes as she felt the sun warm her face and the breeze brush against her skin like a gentle caress. *God truly did work wondrous miracles,* she marveled.

"Is my little boy normally good company on your walks?" Jacob asked in his gruff, deep voice as they resumed walking down a dirt path in the fields.

"Oh, yes. He is ever such good company. Aren't you, Adam?" She said the last part to the playful baby in the carriage who was much more alert and inquisitive than he had been when she had first taken over as his caretaker. He was able to crawl and babble a little more now, something Kayla was looking forward to seeing more of. It made her long for children of her own, something she should have been thinking about with Stephen and yet...

"I'm glad," Jacob replied, interrupting her thoughts. "I've wondered a lot about how I would have managed to cope through everything over the last year if you had not stepped in when you did. I owe you an enormous debt of gratitude, Kayla."

Kayla scoffed in return and shook her head. "You owe me nothing, Jacob," she told him firmly. "I have thoroughly enjoyed every second I've spent with Adam and you."

"And me?" he asked, his tone surprised.

"Oh, well..." Kayla trailed off, her eyes wide as she realized that she had said too much. "Well, we've become friends, haven't we?" She hoped that she might never let on how she was truly feeling about Jacob, especially since she was still technically promised to Stephen. The thought caused an uncomfortable lump in her throat that she couldn't quite swallow down.

"Yes, friends," he replied with a nod.

The rest of their walk was relatively quiet after that.

***

"Jacob!" Kayla called in a panic as she returned home with Adam one afternoon. "Jacob, are you here?" She pushed the carriage into its usual place in the entryway and pulled Adam free from it. She cuddled him close as anxiety overwhelmed her, her heart beating faster and faster as she raced through the house in search of his father.

"Jacob?"

"In here!" he finally shouted in return. It was coming from the pantry and Kayla didn't hesitate to dart through the rest of the house to get to him. When she did, her eyes were wild and her breathing was frantic.

"Adam's sick!" she exclaimed and held out the child for Jacob to see. "I noticed he had a little bit of a cough this morning when I first arrived, but I didn't think much of it. Then I took him outside for some fresh air and well, it has worsened. He seems to have some kind of fever and his nose is running!"

Jacob's face was unmoved by Kayla's rambling, instead, he was deep in thought. "Okay, Kayla, first thing's first, I need you to calm down," he told her in a firm tone. He placed his hands on both of her shoulders. "Take some deep breaths, okay? Adam is going to be just fine, okay?"

"But what if he...?" Kayla couldn't finish the sentence. She shook her head and tears welled in her eyes. "After Lauren, I don't want him to..."

"God decides when it is everyone's time, Kayla," Jacob reassured her with a kind smile. "You know that. However, I'm certain today is not Adam's day." He rubbed his thumbs over her shoulder in a comforting pattern. "Now, I want you to go and sit down with him in the living room while I get some remedies together for our sickly little soldier, okay?"

Our? Kayla couldn't distract herself from the world. For a moment, it felt like this was true. That Adam was her and Jacob's baby. That they were a family, but that wasn't the case was it? She dispelled those thoughts and instead nodded at Jacob before obeying his wishes.

As she sank into the plush sofa, Kayla cradled Jacob close and pulled the blanket around his body away and tossed it to one side. She pressed the back of her hand to his forehead and it felt scorching. Tears ran unbidden down her cheeks leaving wet trails in their wake.

Before she could dwell on Adam's state for too long, Jacob had returned cradling jars and cups of various substances. Kayla watched as Jacob began to rub translucent liquid onto the tiny child's temples and feet. Then he fed Adam a spoonful of a fragrant tea Kayla didn't quite recognize.

When he was finished, Jacob stroked his son's blossoming head of hair and smiled down at him. "He'll be right as rain soon enough. We just need to give him time."

Kayla's mouth dropped open. "How can you know that?" she questioned. "What did you give him?"

Jacob smirked. "A little apple cider vinegar on his temples and feet, then a little thyme made into a tea. It's an old family recipe. It always worked for my ma when we were little. The only time it ever failed to work was…" He trailed off and sighed, looking down at the floor.

"Lauren," Kayla finished for him with a nod of her head. "I'm sorry again, Jacob."

"It's alright, Kayla. God has a plan for us all." As he spoke, Jacob took one of Kayla's hands and held it tight. "Sometimes it's not always clear right away, but I have faith he knows what he's doing."

Electricity thrummed in her veins from his touch and Kayla wondered for the first time if Jacob might feel the same way she did…

***

Just as winter settled in, Jacob had begun to craft a beautiful rocking horse for his son out of a large tree trunk that had been felled in the fall. It was fascinating to watch and as Kayla sat in the armchair of the Raber's house with baby Adam snoozing in her arms, she found her gaze drawn to the baby's father. He was carving the wood out in their back garden where the noise would not disturb the child and the mess could be more easily contained which made Kayla's staring even more illicit.

She shouldn't even be thinking about the way he rolled his sleeves up and revealed the straining muscles of his forearms or the way the perspiration clung to his forehead before beading into drops of sweat and cascading down his strong cheekbones. Yet, she was. Their relationship had developed with ease and little effort into something comfortable and familiar. After spending so much time with the boys,

Kayla was beginning to dread the day when they might not need her anymore.

As she contemplated this, her longing gaze on Jacob became melancholy and her thoughts turned sour. How could she do this to Lauren's memory? She shouldn't be having lustful thoughts for the man who her best friend had married and started a family with. Yet, Kayla was and everything felt so terribly confusing.

Breaking her out of her thoughts, Kayla heard the backdoor slam shut and she realized she had no longer been staring out at Jacob since he wasn't there anymore. She glanced down to the baby to ensure he was still sleeping peacefully before she stood and took him over to the Moses basket where she gently laid him down.

Just as she did so, Jacob rounded the corner with a cloth in his hand. He swiped at the sweat on his brow and looked over at Kayla with narrowed eyes. "Did I catch you watching me, Kay?"

The nickname caught her off guard. He had used it a few times since their friendship had blossomed, but it was still strange. The only people who had ever felt close enough to her to use it had been Lauren and Stephen—the same very two people she would be betraying if she let her thoughts become anything more than thoughts.

"Oh," she replied a little dumbly. "Yes, yes, I was. I was thinking about the rocking horse you're making for Adam." The lie felt bitter and uncomfortable on her tongue as she spoke it, but Kayla knew it was for the best. Circumstances had thrown the two together and that was all this was: feelings borne of close proximity.

"I could always show you a little woodworking sometime if you like," Jacob offered with a smile as he crept closer and leaned over the crib to watch his sleeping son.

"That's men's work."

"There's no harm in you learning a little bit," Jacob countered as he took off his jacket and dropped it over the chair nearest to him.

"Besides, it's about time I repay you for everything you've done for me and Adam these last few months."

Kayla turned, her expression shocked. "You don't need to repay me!" she protested, her hackles rising at even the thought of it. "I haven't helped you with the desire for recompense, Jacob. I am your neighbor and I treat you as I would like to be treated myself."

Jacob smiled and reached forward, his fingers grasping the lock of brunette hair which had freed itself from her bonnet and stretched outward in an unruly fashion. He tucked it behind her ear again, his fingers brushing against the sensitive skin of her neck as he did so. Kayla had to resist a shiver.

"Well then, Kay, I'll be forever grateful for all your help," he told her with a sincere look in his sapphire eyes. Their gaze locked for a moment with their faces so close Kayla thought she could feel his breath on her face. Everything was silent. Adam did not even stir as they stared at one another.

Then, the improbable happened. Jacob's lips moved closer to her own and...

Knock, knock, knock.

A thud on the door snapped Kayla out of her trance and she abruptly stepped away. "I'll just go see who that is!"

When Kayla pulled the door open, she was perplexed to see a red-faced Stephen waiting behind it. "Stephen? What are you doing here?"

"Is he here?" Stephen seethed, pushing roughly past Kayla as he made his way into the house. "Jacob! Come out here you coward!"

"Stephen, the baby is asleep, please keep your voice down," Kayla urged.

"Oh, that's what you care about, is it?" he snapped, taking a step forward and towering over her. "It's alright for you over here playing happy families every day, but what about me? Do you know what the other townsfolk say about you? About me? They say I'm a fool for staying with a woman who is clearly in love with another man!"

Kayla's whole face burned in embarrassment as Stephen accused her of the exact sin she had almost partaken in just moments ago. His proximity was intimidating and Kayla took a step back until her back hit the wall behind her. "Stephen, please, let's talk about this rationally—"

"Rationally?" he spat, taking a step forward to invade her personal space once more. "Are you not even going to deny it, Kay?"

"That's quite enough, Stephen," Jacob cautioned in a deep and firm voice from the doorway to the living room. "Step away from the lady and we won't have any trouble."

Stephen let out an ugly laugh and his face twisted maliciously. "Of course, you're going to come defend her," he barked and turned his attention from Kayla to Jacob. "A knight in shining armor, is that what you are, Jacob? Or are you just looking for someone to warm your bed now your wife's in the ground?"

"Stephen!" Kayla exclaimed, shocked at his brashness.

"What Kay and I do with our own lives is our business," Jacob told him as he stepped closer. "And if you say one more disgusting thing, I won't just kick you out of my house, I'll inform your father of your despicable nature."

Stephen ground his teeth together and then spat on the floor. "You deserve each other," he told them with a snarl before turning on his feet and stomping out of the house, slamming the door hard enough for one of the hinges to break as he left.

After a moment or two, Kayla finally let all the air rush out of her lungs. Her heart raced. She had never been so terrified in her life before. She didn't think Stephen had it in him to be so cruel and mean, but then she wondered if she had ever truly known him at all.

"Are you okay?" Jacob asked, rushing to her side.

"Yes," she answered, her voice shaking a little. "I just never expected... Stephen wasn't like this before..."

"Before me?"

Kayla's eyes met his and verdant green stared into depthless, ocean blue. Her mouth dried up as she tried to come up with a response, but it was futile. Kayla didn't know what to say anymore. Of course, she knew she had feelings for Jacob, but that was wrong. Everyone in the town would gossip about them and she'd be betraying her best friend's memory... wouldn't she?

"Kay, I need to know," Jacob implored, his gaze never breaking from her. "Do you have feelings for me? Stronger than just being friends?"

All of a sudden, Kayla was lost for words. Staring into the eyes of the man she knew now that she loved and feeling uncertain whether she should tell him was the most heartbreaking thing she had ever felt. Her eyes began to water and she opened her mouth to say something, but nothing came out.

"You can talk to me, Kay," Jacob told her and took hold of her hand in his. "We've been through so much together. You helped me through the darkest time in my life. Adam and I have been blessed by your kindness time and time again. I'm sorry I'm asking for more from you yet again, but I want to know if you'd consider joining our family. If you've grown to love me the same way I've grown to love you."

Kayla burst into tears then, overwhelmed with emotion. "Yes, yes," she sobbed, "Jacob, I love you and Adam with all my heart. I never wanted to take Lauren's place, but I do want to be in your lives. I thought I would be betraying her by doing that, but now I realize that all she would want is for us to be happy. I don't think she'd be mad. Do you?"

Jacob smiled down at her and shushed her. "Dry your eyes, Kay," he told her in a soft, gentle voice. "Lauren could never be mad at you. You were her very best friend all her life. You were practically sisters. She would want you to be happy."

"Do you really think so?"

Jacob reached out and pulled Kayla close to his chest and hugged her tight. "I don't think, I know."

Kayla wept for a little while longer before she wrapped her arms around Jacob in return and buried her head into his warm chest. This was everything she had wanted and sought for so long now that she almost couldn't believe it was happening. She let out a sigh and took in a deep breath in an attempt to still the rapid thud of her heart.

"What do we do now?" she asked as a million questions about their situation ran through her head. "Do we get married? Do I move in here? What should we do about Stephen? What will our families think? What if—"

"Hush, Kay. You think too much. All we have to do now is whatever makes us happy and makes our Lord proud," he stated and pulled away just enough to look down at her.

"You make it sound so simple," Kayla protested.

"Life is simple, Kay. You live, you grow, and you love. Right now, I'm concentrating in the love part." He smiled before leaning down and pressing his lips to hers for the very first time. Kayla savored the warmth of him and the way his breath tasted of coffee.

From that day forward, both Kayla and Jacob would be concentrating on love together.

*****

My Amish Roots

Nicola Meyer

Chapter 1

Haylee lay in the darkness of her room staring out of the window at the moon that hung low in the sky, her only consort in her lonely life. Four years after meeting Jase, her heart was broken into a million pieces and scattered across the vast expanse of her own insignificant universe. Move on, they said, he's not worth it, they said, you deserve better. What did they know? None of her so called friends could ever imagine how she felt deep down and how utterly destroyed she was when she walked in on Jase in the arms of her best friend, Lucile. Of course the first thing both of them shouted when caught in the act was – it's not what you think!

After Jase pleaded with her and Lucile convinced her that it was an irresponsible judgement error on her part and that it would never happen again, she gave it another shot. She should have known better. Naïve little Haylee, who only tries to see the good in people ended up as the biggest fool of them all and when it happened a second time, she could no longer be ignorant. It was obvious that between the chemical combination of Lucile's raging pheromones and Jase's ego boosted testosterone, she never stood a chance. She had to finally admit to herself that she was never going to find true love, and friendships are feeble pastimes for pre-schoolers.

It's been almost two months since her relationship with Jase ended, and it wasn't long after that, that she also handed in her resignation as an article clerk. Breaking up with Jase and seeing him once in a blue moon she could handle well, but working with him and sharing the same open office day in and day out was a little too much to handle. It amazed her how men in could be so callous and move on without a worry in the world. She had managed thus far, but the more she sat at home she started to feel cooped up like a bird in a too small cage.

She sighed and tugged her blanket over her shoulders and tucked it under her chin as she turned onto her other side, this time staring at her graduation photo. She stood tall and proud, alone in her toga with her rolled up certificate in her hand, no immediate family to share her successes with her. Her adoptive mother had passed away six months short of her graduation that year. Haylee sniffed and blinked away the tears. She didn't cry then and she won't cry now. Finally giving up on sleeping she tossed the blanket back and sat up in bed. Her mom always told her, that every person has left something behind in their past, that sits there and waits until they go back to find it and resolve it. And until recently she had never thought she wanted to go back there. She was only four when she was adopted, a lonely gray mouse stuck in foster care. From the first day she arrived at her new family, she was accepted and spoiled rotten. She never needed for anything in her life, and she never felt as if she was any different to any of the other kids, so why she suddenly felt like digging out the past was a mystery to her, but every day it became more and more pressing. And here at two in the morning, she was stuck between forcing herself to sleep or logging into her email to see if the adoption agency managed to track down her biological mother or family. Insomnia won the battle and she finally made herself a cup of coffee and sat down at her desk and logged into her emails.

Dear Miss Jones

We have managed to track down your biological mother, but it is with regret that we inform you that she passed away a few years ago due to illness. We have however managed to track down her parents, your grandparents. We do however wish that you consider the fact that they may not...

Hayley stared at the email, reading it over and over again, somehow grief evaded her, and it was like reading the sad story of a stranger. What she did learn from this was that her mother was born Amish, and that her grandparents lived in an Amish community in Ethridge, Tennessee. But even if she knew who they were, what good would that do now? It wasn't as if she could reunite with her long lost mother anymore. But what she might be able to figure out is what type of woman her mother was and what type of life she lived. Maybe it will even shed some light on why her mother gave her up for adoption. As she spent her time reading up on the Amish and their culture, it became more and more evident that her mother may not have had a choice, but this was pure speculation. And unless she took the time to find these things out for herself, she would always be guessing about the woman who brought her into this world.

Besides, it wasn't as if she had anything better to do with her time. She had no job, no love life and no coffee, she thought as she looked at the empty canister in front of her.

That was it; she was going to take the last of her savings and head to Ethridge and find the Lapp's.

Chapter 2

The whole way to Ethridge, Hayley kept wondering if she was making a mistake. She was about to embark on a journey she was in the least bit prepared for. Before she left everything behind, she made effort to reinvent her wardrobe with a few modest outfits just so that she wouldn't look too outrageous amongst the Amish. But even now as she sat in the back of the cab, her heart was beating a million miles a second and she was on the verge of having a nervous breakdown. She had just left behind the only life she knew, not that there was much left of her for her to salvage, but she was somewhat comfortable where she was.

The cab pulled into the small town of Ethridge and stopped in front of what appeared to be a touring business.

"This is as far as I can go," the cab driver said and pointed to this meter.

Hayley nodded and fished for cash to pay the cab driver and the moment her bags were offloaded and she stood like a singled out deer in hunting season outside on the sidewalk she wanted to burst out in tears. Whatever was she thinking coming out here?

"Hello, may I help you?"

Startled Hayley nearly lost her balance as she spun to look at the stranger behind her, "Oh-I-um, well, I'm looking for someone," she said and dug in her purse, "Mr. and Mrs. Lapp?"

"Oh Fredrick and Mary Lapp, yah, they live here. I can take you," the young man said.

"You know them?" Hayley asked in disbelief.

"Yah, well it's a small community we all know each other," he said tucking his thumbs under his suspenders.

Hayley couldn't help but stare, wondering if all Amish men were this good looking. This guy couldn't be much older than her twenty-five. And although he was dressed modestly in what she had to assume Amish clothes, he looked reasonably attractive.He had ebony black hair with willow green eyes set deeply in his skull.

"If you're done staring..." he said interrupting her thoughts with his brows drawn together.

Embarrassingly she shook her head, "I'm so sorry, I just... it has been a really long day and I've traveled a long way."

"No matter, my name is Duncan," he said and nodded his head courteously, extending his hand.

"Hayley," she said and gave his hand an overly firm shake.

"Well I best be getting you to the Lapp's, the weather is turning foul."

Without notice he started loading her luggage into a carriage that stood nearby and then patted the back of the carriage, indicating her seat.

Who was she to ask questions, she hadn't the foggiest about their customs and every website she visited to learn about them were know-it-all windbags who have made up assumptions. So instead of opposing she hopped into the back of the carriage and sat down.

"So do you know the Lapps?" Duncan called over his shoulder as they made their way into the town.

"I...sort of, actually, I knew their daughter," she lied, she had no clue what their daughter was like. Just because Hannah Lapp gave birth to her, didn't exactly mean she knew her.

"I think you might have them mistaken for someone different, they only have a son, but Kendrick moved to Lancaster with his wife."

Well, this was a good start, she thought as she tucked her lip under her teeth, "Perhaps I am confused, but I suppose there is no harm in meeting them. Maybe they might know Hannah Lapp as extended family."

"Hannah Lapp," Duncan repeated, "The name sounds familiar."

The carriage came to a halt and Hayley fell forward along with her luggage and just then the heavens opened up.

"Come!" Duncan called and reached for a sheet to cover her luggage before effortlessly lifting her off the wagon and placing her on her feet, "The Lapp's live here. If you hurry I can wait and take you back to Richland Inn."

"Wait, what do you mean back to town, I need to be here in Ethridge," she protested as Duncan lead her up to the house where the Lapps lived.

"Well if the Lapps won't let you stay in their home, you have nowhere else to stay, unless you want to sleep in the barn."

"The barn?" she asked appalled.

"Duncan, vas in der velt?" an elderly man interrupted as he opened his door.

Duncan immediately removed his hat and clutched it in front of him then looked at her before turning his attention back to the older man.

"Mister Lapp, this is Hayley. She's come to Ethridge to look for..."

Before Duncan could continue Hayley stepped up and extended her hand, "Grandfather?"

The older man's complexion paled, and he exchanged looks with Duncan then looked at Hayley, "You're mistaken," he mumbled and moved to close the door, but then an elderly woman appeared and the expression on her face was one of pure shock.

"Hannah... you look just like her," she said in a trembling voice as her eyes shot full of tears.

"Grandmother?" Haylee said as she stood with her hands folded in front of her.

"Come, you're going to get soaking wet out in the rain," she said as she dragged Hayley into the house, despite her Grandfather's disapproval.

And as she disappeared into the kitchen she heard her grandfather mumble for Duncan to bring her luggage inside.

Her grandparents, she couldn't believe it. She was actually in the very house her biological mother grew up in. Her grandmother seemed far more accepting of her than her grandfather did, but she refused to make any assumptions until she had all the facts. For now, she will take the time she had to get to know them.

Chapter 3

A week since her arrival and all she could determine was that her mother, Hanna Lapp went on a Rumspringa and never returned.

"Did she never write to you?" Hayley asked her grandmother one morning after her grandfather left to go to work.

"She wrote to us, but only ever to let us know she was fine," her grandmother said softly as she continued with her sewing.

"But weren't you in the least bit worried?"

Mary put down her sewing and reached out for Hayley's hand, "Yah, we were worried, especially your grandfather, but our laws are different to those on the outside. Hannah made her choice and she had a chance to return."

Hayley sat quietly for a moment and squeezed her grandmother's hand. The short while she had been here in the Amish community of Ethridge, she had found a sense of peace and tranquillity she never felt before. With the exception of a minority of locals who walked wide circles around her, the younger people like her were friendly and very accommodating. She couldn't understand why her mother would have left for good, and trade this life for what lay outside in the world. But then, being on holiday in a strange place was far different that living the life in full.

A knock on the door drew her attention and her grandmother quickly set her sewing aside and went to open the door, and a few seconds later she returned with Duncan in tow.

"Hayley, Duncan is here to see you," her grandmother said smiling.

Duncan was another person she was growing fond of at an alarming rate, but thankfully the walls she erected around herself kept her level headed. She knew that the only reason she felt closer to him than any of the others was that he was the first person she met when she arrived.

"Hi Duncan, what a nice surprise," she said standing up.

"Good day to you Hayley," he nodded tucking his thumbs in his suspenders, "I was wondering if you would like to go to the market today, I have a few errands to run."

Hayley felt the slight flutter of butterflies in her stomach and tugged her hand into her midriff. It would be rather nice to get out a little and get to know other parts of the community, she thought and then nodded.

"It would be lovely, let me get my coat and purse," she said and hurried to her room.

She forced herself not to eavesdrop on her grandmother' and Duncan's conversation and quickly got what she needed before joining them.

In no time they were on the carriage and on their way to the market, this time Hayley got to sit in the front and not like some baggage on the back.

"So how are you enjoying your stay here in Ethridge?" Duncan asked curiously.

"It's nice. I mean, it's very different to city life, but so far I'm enjoying the peace and quiet," she said and glanced out over the landscape.

"Yah, it's very quiet. So did you manage to find out about Hannah?"

"A little," she said.

She didn't want to put the Lapps in any sort of disrepute, but she found it hard to believe that Duncan had no clue about her, but then again, he was probably still a baby when Hannah left the Amish community.

"So will you be moving on then?" he said clearing his throat.

Hayley turned to look at him and smiled, "Not sure, maybe. Tell me about this Rumspringa thing."

Duncan laughed and looked at her, "Well, Rumspringa means to run around, when the youngsters turn sixteen they can choose to go out and experience things outside of our community. It's each one's choice, some do it and some don't."

"Did you ever, I mean did you do it when you turned sixteen?" she asked curiously.

"Nay, I never did. I have all I need right here."

"So you never wonder what lies out in the cities."

Duncan drew the carriage to a halt and then turned to look at Hayley, studying her with those intense willow green eyes.

"Most young men leave because they are not satisfied with their life here, mostly because they are tempted by the modern world, and women," he said, his cheeks growing rosy.

Hayley tried to hide her smile and coughed softly, "So you never wanted to go find some hanky-panky?"

"Hanky -panky?" Duncan asked and blinked, "What is that?"

"Uh... well meeting women, dating and so on."

Duncan threw his head back and laughed, "Oh no, I had no interest in those things. Not then anyway," he said and then tugged on the reins sending the horse back onto the road, "I always believed that at the right time God will send the right woman my way. I'm a patient man Hayley Jones."

When he looked at her then, she felt her heart flutter in her chest and she immediately looked the other way. Her mind was clearly playing tricks on her; there was no way that Duncan would even consider looking at her twice. She was an outsider for one, and secondly, she wasn't exactly a virgin either. And although she still knew very little about their laws and traditions, she was sure the Amish probably had the highest moral values in the world second to nuns.

The rest of their trip was in silence, and a few miles further they finally reached the Amish Country Mall. Hayley was quite surprised by the variety of goods that were sold at this place, but more so how many non-Amish visited the place. It was a tourist distraction for curious people. And as she stood next to Duncan and the Carriage in her own authentic Amish dress, a sense of pride washed over her. Surprised that she actually felt Amish in some far-fetched way, she smiled at Duncan and then headed into the shop. She found it quite amusing that it was called a Mall when all it really had were old antique trinkets and a limited menu of food. There were some items for sale but it was hardly considered anything close to a shopping mall. When she exited the store she found Duncan standing next to her grandfather, both in deep conversation. Instead of barging in on them she took a walk around the store to give them their own time. Her grandfather had hardly spoken a word to her since her arrival and he was still a great big mystery to her. On occasion when she did ask her gran about him, she simply avoided the topic. She wasn't any closer to find out exactly why her mother never came back.

Chapter 4

Duncan couldn't help but admire Hayley, and although she was an outsider, she seemed to adapt quite well to the Amish life. It's been two weeks since he met her, and the more time he spent with her the more he started to like her. The first day he saw her was the first time he ever really looked at a woman. She was modestly dressed in a floral print dress that flowed elegantly down her body to her calves, but what intrigued him most was her shyness. The fact that he had the impulsive need to run his fingers through her long brown tresses was abnormal for him and he quickly stifled that need, by reminding himself that she was an outsider, which helped.

Normally when outsiders visited the Amish communities they stuck to their modern clothes, where the women wore as little as possible. No wonder so many of the Amish boys opted to go on their expedition to the cities, being tempted by the promises that the modern world presented. Two of his own best friends went out to experience the world and all it had to offer, but he never felt that desire or pull to know what happens out there. He was more than content to live this life of simplicity, working on the farm and making goat's cheese. There were many times when he attended the sings and where he contemplated the option of taking a wife, but none of the girls here in Ethridge ever made him feel the way he did now. And he was adamant that if he was going to take a wife, it would be someone who would completely consume his thoughts. He wanted the same love with a wife than his mother and father shared. He had never seen them argue, and they always showed their affection towards each other. And if they could have such a devoted marriage, why could he not have the same?

Duncan was caught in his own thoughts when the smell of burning wood and grass wafted through the air.

"Duncan!" It was Hayley who rode towards him on one of the Lapp's horses, her eyes wide, "Come quick, my grandfather's barn is on fire!" she cried.

In an instant, Duncan had called his father and his neighbors, and everyone else he could alert and they were on their way by carriage to the Lapp's farmlands. Up ahead he could see the plume of fire explode into the gray sky. Flames rolled outwards and embers were flying up into the sky.

When he pulled up next to Hayley where she dismounted the horse, he took the reins and handed it to another young man, "Take the horse to my father's barn and keep it there," he instructed and then turned to Hayley, "What happened?"

"I have no idea, we were all having dinner when we heard the loud crash of lightning, and not long after that the smoke was everywhere," she said ringing her hands together.

Duncan's concern for Hayley had to be set aside, and although he wanted to comfort her, he had to attend to the bigger problem.

"Okay, go to the house and stay inside," he ordered as he scooped a bucket of water from the trough.

"But I can help," she protested and reached for a small barrel.

"You've done enough, now go and sit with your grandmother, I'm sure she could use the company."

Her mouth opened in protest but then shut, and with a slight nod, she ran across the field towards the house.

They fought all night to get the fire under control, thankfully the Lord had blessed them with rain to help put the fire out, but all that was left were the charred remains of the barn in the smoky morning air that reeked of burnt wood and straw. His father had warned Fredrick about the tall dead tree that stood so close to the barn. But misfortune led to lighting striking the dead tree and causing it to fall on to the barn. Luckily it was only the barn that burned down, somehow the horses were freed before the barn was completely on fire, and he has the slightest suspicion that it was Hayley's quick thinking that saved the animals. As for the equipment, it was all replaceable.

"Thank you, son, if you didn't arrive when you did I would have lost all my horses," Mr. Lapp said as he came to stand next to Duncan.

"Nay, that was not my doing. Hayley saved the horses," he said and looked at the older man.

"Hayley saved them?" he asked disbelievingly.

"Yah, she came to fetch me on horseback, I've never seen a woman ride so well, but she came to call me straight away. By the time I got here the horses were already in the fields and Kent took them to my barn."

Fredrick stood quietly for a while rubbing his chin, and Duncan knew that he had his own demons to face. He too had never heard of Hannah Lapp, but spending time with Hayley he had learned a great deal.

"She's seeking your approval," Duncan said crossing his arms as both of them looked at what remained of the barn, "She deserves a fair chance."

"You're right," Fredrick said and then headed towards the house.

Duncan looked as the older man walked away, his shoulders hunched as if he carried a heavy burden, but he knew Hayley deserved a fair chance, she had nothing to do with her mother's disobedience or her choice to give her up for adoption.

Later that day, Duncan stood in his father's barn, grooming the Lapps' horses. The least he could do was make sure that none of them were injured. But more than anything he needed to keep busy so that he could chase the thoughts of Hayley from his mind. Every waking hour was seemingly consumed by thoughts of her, and after her courageous act it was even worse. Now he knew exactly how King Solomon must have felt, being tempted by a beautiful woman.

"Duncan?" he heard Hayley's voice from outside the barn.

"In here!" he answered and tossed the brush in the sack hanging on the wall.

"Oh there you are," she said smiling and held out a basket for him, "Grandma and I baked these to thank you for helping us out with the horses."

Duncan smiled and took the basket filled with cookies, "Thanks, but I think you deserve all the credit, if it wasn't for you these horses would be charred with the barn."

He noticed Hayley blush as she averted her eyes, "I love horses, I had to do something."

Duncan stepped closer and reached out to tuck his finger under her chin, "And you did an amazing job of saving them," he said but his voice betrayed him.

This close to her, he could smell the fresh scent of lavender and vanilla, and although it was just the crook of his finger brushing her unblemished skin under her chin, it was the silk soft smoothness that tempted him more than anything. And without a second thought, he stepped in and pressed his lips against hers. Hers were soft, like cotton pillows and although the kiss was brief, it was a defying moment for him. He knew there and then that Hayley was the woman he'd been waiting for all these years.

He broke the chaste kiss but didn't step away from her; instead he kept his eyes locked on hers. It was that moment between two people where words were irrelevant syllables and consonants were fleeting sounds that would never be able to express the emotions that sparked between them.

It was Hayley that stepped away first, and how shyly tucked a strand of hair behind her ear.

"My grandfather said that they will be doing a barn rising this coming weekend, will you come?" she asked softly.

"I wouldn't miss it for the world," Duncan said.

And as Hayley walked back out of the Barn she looked back over at him again and smiled.

Duncan felt like a teenager for the first time, and now more than ever was he determined to make Hayley Jones his wife.

Chapter 5

The barn raising was well on its way, the men from the community had spent most of the morning working and Hayley was amazed by how quickly the barn started taking shape. She heard many stories about this experience and how the Amish are able to build an entire barn in one day, but she had never seen it with her own eyes. Duncan was at the front line of everything. He did the planning and the design, his skill as a builder came in handy and it appeared that young to old admired him, but not nearly as much as she did.

When she first decided to come to Ethridge, finding love was the last thing she anticipated. After her failed engagement to Jase, she had sworn off on ever dating again, but here she was, utterly captivated by Duncan. He was the complete opposite to Jase. He was kind, considerate, a true gentleman and there was something about him that she craved.

"He's a fine young man," her gran said as she handed her the basket of fresh fruit.

Hayley tore her eyes away from the barn and smiled at her gran, "Yes, he is," she admitted.

"You know, Hannah never told us about you until after she gave you up for adoption," her grandmother started, "When she told us your grandfather begged her to withdraw the adoption and rather send you to us."

Hayley sat down opposite her gran at the wooden table, "So you did know about me?"

"Oh yes we did, but your mother had already handed you to your new parents, and we had no way of finding you. That day you arrived here in Ethridge, you were a spitting image of my Hannah."

Hayley's eyes shot full of tears and she reached out to take her grandmother's hand, "My adopted parents were good people, they really looked after me as if I was their own."

"I know, but I can't help wonder just how things would have been if Hannah had come back home," the older woman admitted and lowered her eyes.

"I'm here now though, and you've made me feel at home."

"Yah, yah, I know. I've been trying my best. Your grandfather blames himself for what happened, but he's a good man."

Hayley smiled and then looked back at the men toiling in the sun. Her grandfather was a proud but humble man, and she knew that deep down he cared for her.

By six o'clock that evening, the barn stood tall in all its glory. Brand spanking new as if no disaster had struck it just a week ago, and everyone in the community had gathered to celebrate the event. It was a festive atmosphere and for the first time in her life Hayley felt as if she belonged. Over the weeks she spent here in Ethridge learning to bake and quilt, she hardly thought of her life in the city. And the hustle and bustle of peak hour traffic and busy shopping malls were nothing but a distant memory of a temporary life she once knew.

She made a few friends and even the older people had started to like her. Maybe it was due to the fact that she did not come here to dispute their faith or their ways, but she embraced it like any Amish citizen would.

From across the group of people, she caught Duncan looking at her. But instead of looking away, she smiled at him, and even when one of his friends tapped him on his shoulder he still looked her way, refusing to drop his glance. The sight of him made her knees weak. She had to force herself to look away before her grandfather came to sit beside her.

"My dear," he started sounding uncomfortable, "I owe you an apology for my behavior."

Hayley turned to her grandfather and smiled, "No need, you had a lot to cope with, with my untimely arrival. I should have taken better care to notify you before I just dropped in."

"No, it's not that. I-I never gave your mother a chance to rectify things and for that, I am forever guilty, I should have gone to find her."

Fredrick pinched the bridge of his nose and shut his eyes and Hayley knew he was fighting back the tears, she gently placed her hand on his, "The choices we make are our own, and we are all responsible for them, no one can take responsibility for the mistakes of others."

There was a moment of silence, and when her grandfather looked up at her again he smiled tenderly, "You will make a wonderful Amish woman," he said and patted her hand, "And Duncan would choose well to ask for your hand."

"Hayley, come!" One of the girls called and tugged her up by her hand, "You must join in on the sing."

Before Hayley could process the words of her grandfather she was caught smack bang in the middle with a bunch of the younger people, and although there were no instruments, the clapping of hands and the harmonies of voices made the songs come to life. Among the crowd was Duncan, subtly making his way closer to her and the closer he came the more her heart beat out of control and the butterflies that hijacked her insides fluttered up a storm. She might very well be an outsider but she could not deny the fact that somehow Providence had claimed a victory.

"Would you spare me a few minutes of your time?" Duncan whispered as he reached her.

"Of course," she said and followed him outside.

Duncan had his hands tucked in his pockets as he stood outside. The moonlight spilled down from the heavens like a silver curtain, bathing their surroundings in silver dust and casting its subtle glow over them. And as Hayley came to stand next to him, they both glanced up at the sky.

"Hayley..."

"Duncan..."

They started at the same time and then burst out laughing.

"You first," Hayley insisted and Duncan smiled and turned towards her.

"Okay, well, I'm sure this will come as no surprise to you, but I thought it best I clear the air," he started clutching his hand in his hands, "I think or rather, I know that I have grown very fond of you, and I know that it may be a little more complicated than usual, but I have spoken to your grandfather."

Hayley stood playing with the string of her prayer cap, coiling it around her index finger nervously. It felt as if her heart was going to jump out of her throat as Duncan went on, explaining how he had asked her grandfather if he would allow him to court her. A few weeks ago, she would never have considered this, but now where she stood under the moonlit sky, with her hand in Duncan's she knew exactly what she wanted.

"And did my grandfather approve?" she asked curiously biting her lip.

"He did indeed, which is why I have gathered to courage to ask you in person," he admitted and smiled.

Hayley shifted her weight and sucked in a breath, she had no idea how Amish dating customs worked. Of all the things she had yet to learn, dating hardly featured and she recalled only briefly spot reading over that section.

"So are we going to be bundling?" she asked innocently and blushed.

Duncan raised his brows and chuckled, "My dear Hayley, you have so much to learn still, no one does that anymore," he said and stepped closer to her and reached to remove her prayer cap.

"Is that allowed?" She whispered softly as Duncan's lips hovered over hers and he pulled the pin that secured her hair in a bun lose.

"What happens between us, and the Lord, is all that matters," he said and then wrapped her loose braid around his hand and kissed her fully on the lips.

Chapter 6

Hayley stood in front of the mirror, while her grandmother fussed with her long hair. It's been a year since she joined the community and although her and Duncan's feelings for each other were no secret to the rest of the community, they both kept their word to follow the rules and customs as required by the Amish Council.

"So the food is almost ready. Once your Grandfather and I are off to the church service, you and Duncan can sit down and celebrate your betrothal."

Hayley looked in the reflection of the mirror at her grandmother, the woman she had grown to love and smiled, "Do you think I will make him happy, Grossmammi?" she asked.

"Natuurlijk! You're his future and the woman he had been waiting for all this time," her gran reassured her.

After her grandparents left to go to church, where the minister would be announcing the brides to be, she waited patiently at the house for Duncan to arrive. She kept looking at the clock on the wall, it was a unique hand crafted clock made especially for her by Duncan, as a courtship gift. Time seemed like it had deliberately slowed down, and when she heard the carriage finally pull up in front of the house, she had to force herself to stay calm and not rush into his arms. Other than the first time he kissed her, and the second and the third, this was probably one of the most amazing moments in her life. After tonight, she would officially be engaged, and by October, only two months away, she would be Mrs. Hayley Beiler.

"You do know that you still have a choice right?" Duncan said much later after they had finished dessert.

"I have made my choice, and it is to stay here with you," she said smiling.

They were seated on a wooden bench outside on the porch; waiting for the Lapp's to arrive.

"Are you a hundred percent sure?" he asked again, this time lacing his fingers with hers.

Hayley turned to him and placed her free hand over their entwined fingers. The past few months she had made the effort to learn their various customs, do bible study, get familiar with their laws, but she knew beyond anything that her life was here with him.

"Duncan, I am happy and I would not change this for anything," she said and then leaned close enough for her lips to brush his, "Ich liebe dich," she whispered and gave him a chaste kiss on his lips.

"And I love you, Hayley Jones," Duncan said, smiling from ear to ear and then quoted Songs of Solomon, "You are altogether beautiful, my darling, beautiful in every way."

~*~

Most of all, let love guide your way. Col 3:14

THE BIG AMISH ADVENTURE

ERICA FANNING

103

It was a beautiful, sunny day in the little community where Joshua Miller lived, and he was excited about this particular day. He was taking his little sister, Miriam, to her first Rumspringa event. Since Joshua was the eldest son of the Miller family, he had the pleasure of taking the younger siblings to their different functions in the family buggy. From where the Miller's lived the church was on the other side of the community, which happened to have a 2-lane highway that went through for the Englishers that lived in the two neighboring towns on either side. Joshua's parents had learned to trust him because he had been able to successfully avoid an accident with cars on more than one occasion, but they seemed to be unsure now because Miriam would be with him.

"It's not you that we don't trust," Mrs. Miller tried to explain. "It's those cars... they're always driving like it's the end of the world. And even after the state changed the speed limit through the community, they still don't really slow down. Please be careful."

"We love you son," Mr. Miller added. "We just want to make sure you and Miriam get back safely and in one piece."

"Don't you worry," Joshua said, confident in his maneuvering abilities. "I will make sure that Miriam and I come back to you the way we left." He smiled reassuringly, which seemed to settle his parents some.

The trek to the church was extremely uneventful. Even Miriam commented that it seemed quiet for a Sunday afternoon.

Maybe going home will be just as easy, Joshua thought to himself. *Especially since it will be later in the evening.*

What nobody counted on was someone asking Miriam on her first night to court him, or at least Joshua didn't count on that. Samuel Stoltzfus was a nice young man that the Miller family had seen a lot of growing up because he had always been interested in Miriam, but somehow it slipped Joshua's mind that he would be there. For Joshua, it was just another night to fellowship with his friends; he wasn't interested in a lot of the young women that were interested in him, and the ones that he would have been interested in were taken already.

"Looks like you'll be going home alone again, Joshua," Samuel poked him as he walked past, leading Miriam to his buggy. Joshua simply smirked and shook his head. He enjoyed not playing the courting game that everyone else seemed to be playing. He wanted to take it slow and let his life play out as smoothly as possible. These days, that included not worrying about another person in his life.

On the way home, Joshua began mapping out the next day in his head. It was a great way to pass the time and that's all that he really had as he guided the trusty steed along the side of the road. As usual, there still weren't many cars around, but a lot of them seemed to be driving dangerously close to Joshua. Secretly, he was glad Miriam went home with Samuel; he hoped they got home safely.

And then it happened. Before he even had a moment to process what was happening, he was thrown from his seat. A sharp pain bit into his leg and he yelled in pain. His head hit a rock and the last thing he remembered someone was emerging from a dark muscle car asking him if he was okay.

He knew he wasn't. *This is the end of life as I know it.*

He awoke slowly. Everything around him seemed white and clean. He had never seen any Plain dwelling like this before.

Where am I?

A woman moved into his vision. Joshua attempted to move his head and thought better of it when a thousand pins and needles shot down his spine. He winced from the pain and something to his right started screaming. The woman—who was wearing dark blue scrubs—quickly moved toward the noise and fiddled with something before the sound stopped and Joshua began to feel better. He opened his mouth to speak, but all that came out was a cough.

"Hello there! How is my favorite patient doing?" The nurse seemed to be yelling at him, as if she thought he was deaf.

"Water," Joshua managed to croak out.

"Sure thing!" The volume hadn't gone down; maybe that's just the way she spoke, he decided.

After he had a few sips and felt he could form a coherent sentence, he asked her where he was.

"Well," the blonde-haired woman began. "You're in the hospital. You've been here for about a week. After your family released you to our care, we had to do some emergency surgery…"

Joshua was confused. "Emergency surgery? On what?" He checked all appendages; hands, arms, legs, feet… Something felt off. His left leg moved just fine, but he couldn't get his right leg to cooperate. After some repositioning, he looked down. Where his right leg should have been, there was simply… nothing.

"I'm so sorry," the nurse said, but Joshua didn't really hear her.

"What happened to my leg? What did you do?" He felt panicked. What was this? All of the pain he felt when he first woke up was suddenly gone as adrenaline took over. "Where is my leg? What did you do?!" Red began to creep into the edges of his vision as loud beeping came from his right. A few large men in white and two more nurses rushed into the room and began holding him down.

"Sir, please calm down." Everyone spoke calmly but firmly, though Joshua didn't hear it.

"How can I live like this? How will I live?"

Panic was the last thing he remembered before sleep overtook his mind completely.

It took a full week of waking up in a panic and having to be sedated before Joshua woke up one day and finally seemed to grasp what had happened. He had lost his leg due to an infection from an accident with a reckless driver and now there was no real future for him in his community.

People won't accept me, he thought bitterly. *I've seen how they treat outsiders. I've seen how they treat the sick. They don't care about them and just want to pretend they don't exist.*

No matter what his family tried to tell him over the next few weeks, he decided he was going to get his own little abode in the community and live on his own. Joshua's father had been looking into it with him before the accident. While Joshua had been in and out of consciousness in the hospital, Mr. Miller and Joshua's younger brother, James had completed it to fit Joshua's new life. Joshua didn't like the way that sounded and instantly decided no matter how nice it was he wasn't going to like it.

A Mennonite friend of Mr. Miller's, Mr. Benjamin, took them from the hospital on the day of Joshua's release to Joshua's new home on the edge of the little community. Since Joshua had such a low expectation of his new home, nothing he saw surprised him or changed his mind. For his father and younger brother, he put on a smile and told them how much he loved it even though he wanted to raze the small dwelling with everything in him. He hopped out of the van with the help of his mother and the hospital-issued crutches.

There is no way my life could be any more humiliating right now, he thought to himself bitterly. *My mother is helping me out of a Mennonite's van, coming from an English hospital because I have only one leg. There is no way I could be more humiliated.*

He was quickly proven wrong as the entire community came to his new home to welcome him back. He knew it was all fake; there was no way he was going to let these people into his life when they didn't want anything to do with him before. He played along for the time. He didn't want to disappoint his mother, who was more than overjoyed at the outpouring of "love" the community was showing not only Joshua, but his entire family. Miriam was already shown a lot of attention because of her blooming relationship with young Samuel Stoltzfus, but Joshua noticed how much the other members—both young and old—showed her more respect. At that moment, Joshua decided he would go along with the love and care he received if that meant his family was shown the same love and care. They deserved it. They worked hard for it.

Joshua just wanted to be left alone. That's all he ever wanted, but for his family he would be the most outgoing person the community had ever known.

A few weeks later, during one of the required physical therapy visits, John, the therapist brought up an interesting proposition to Joshua.

"Mr. Miller," Joshua hated that the young man called him that, but allowed it when it seemed like he really had something on his mind. "I don't normally bring this kind of stuff up... but you don't seem very happy." Joshua sighed. This was one of the rare days that only Joshua was home while John was there.

"You know what, Johnny? I'm not." Joshua decided to just be honest. "I no longer have a leg, I have a community who pretends to love me and a family that doesn't know what to do with me. They gave me this house even after everything because they thought it was best to move on, but really all it does is make me feel farther than ever from them. Because now they have to come to me, and that requires them being on the same road that I was on when my accident happened. I just wish that none of this had ever happened."

John stopped what he was doing and looked Joshua in the eyes. "I can't bring your leg back, but I can do the next best thing. What do you think about this new prosthetic that a doctor friend of mine has been working on? It would almost be like you never even lost your leg."

"Does it take the phantom pain away? Because if not, you can't even make that claim."

"Well," John had a small gleam in his eye. "From the few people I've heard that have used it... yeah." That stopped Joshua.

"Really?" John nodded.

"Obviously, giving you a limb isn't going to fix your relationships, but it will help you get out of the house and start to take your life back. That's a good start, don't you think?"

That question almost seemed rhetorical, so Joshua didn't bother to answer. John went back to helping Joshua with his exercises and the day went along without another incident or mention of this possible new freedom.

For the next two weeks every time John was there—whether someone was there with Joshua or not—Joshua asked about this new prosthetic. Everyday, the pros seemed to outweigh the cons more and more. One day, Mr. Miller confronted Joshua about it after John left.

"Son, do you really want to do this?"

"Dad," Joshua figured there was a lot he was doing that his father didn't know about. He wasn't about to keep calling him Father as if he really honored him. "At this point, I'm practically an invalid. People are always coming over and giving me food as if I can't cook. They bring me blankets as if I don't have a whole extra bedroom full already. I don't need people's sympathy! What I need is to get my life back!"

Joshua didn't realize he was yelling until he really saw the look on his father's face. It was full of shock and hurt. Joshua thought for sure his father would remind him to respect his elders, that he would give him the what-for, that there would be a yelling match. What his father did scared him more than anything that had happened in Joshua's life until this point.

His father simply nodded once, gathered his coat and hat from the rack, and turned back to his son for what would be the last time he would probably ever set foot in Joshua's home again.

"Just know that whatever happens, I will always love you."

With that, Joshua's father was gone. When the door closed behind him, Joshua felt seriously alone for the first time in his life.

Amanda Waller was a petite, young blonde woman straight out of nursing school. She began working for Dr. Jacob Zimmerman, the doctor who had developed the smart prosthetics, the very next day. For her, it was a dream come true. Not only did she have one of the best-paying jobs in the city, but she also got to work with the man she had considered a father figure in her life.

As Amanda was restocking some of the completed prosthetics in the supplies closet, John came in. Although Amanda was not registered as a physical therapist, she had learned a lot from John in the two short months she had worked alongside him. It helped that John had a brand new Amish patient that he could use as an example without having to worry about too many details being spilled to the wrong people. Since Amish people don't have friends outside of their own communities, they never knew what was or wasn't said about them. However, John was very honorable and would never divulge more than was necessary for a good, short lesson in P.T.

"Hi John," Amanda called. She heard John sigh and looked back to see him sitting in a chair with his head in his hands. She immediately left her stocking duties and moved toward him. "What's wrong?"

He looked up at her and shook his head. "I don't understand why I agreed to help an Amish person. They hold themselves back for a religion? A belief? What? I don't understand. And I have the unfortunate privilege of trying to convince this man if he really needs a prosthetic. He's unhappy, Amanda. I want to help him."

"Well if he's unhappy, that's not something you can fix." If anybody knew that, it was Amanda. She had tried to find solace in drugs, alcohol, and sex before fully giving her life to God. She may not have agreed with everything the Amish people did, but she knew there were good people in Amish communities who really loved God. "Sometimes the ones that need help the most are the ones who don't want it."

"But that's the thing," John retorted as Amanda found a chair and sat down next to him. "It's not that he doesn't want it; his family doesn't want him to have it." Amanda shrugged.

"Okay, then he doesn't get it, right?"

"Amanda, he's 20. He is legally old enough to make his own decisions." Amanda had seen photographs of the man, Joshua Miller. He certainly looked like he could pass as 16 on any given day.

"I have an idea," Amanda was about to tread into some unfamiliar waters. "What if maybe he just needs someone different to push him and his family over the edge? If this is something that will at least help him, maybe they just need a different way of looking at things." John looked at her questioningly.

"Are you sure? I mean, I don't want you to get into trouble. And you're not registered as a physical therapist."

"Maybe not, but I have a great teacher." She smiled at him before adding, "Besides, we can consider this a trial run for some field experience. There's only so many supply closets I can stock before we run out of space." They both chuckled.

"I've never really seen Dr. Zimmerman say no to you," John stated after a moment. "I guess we can at least run it by him."

Joshua just wanted to get rid of the pain. He had no family, no friends, no livelihood... and no leg. What else was he to do? His parents would be ashamed if they knew what he did with his days.

There's no way I can tell them what's really going on. There's no hope for me.

The only thing that kept Joshua going was his weekly visits with John and the possibility that he could turn his life around with a prosthetic. He finally decided that the next time John came, he would say yes to this new prosthetic.

There was a knock at the door. Joshua grabbed his crutches and hobbled over. When he opened the door he saw a petite blonde-haired woman, not much taller than five feet with a cute bob, standing before him.

"Hi Joshua," the woman said as if she were a messenger from Gott and knew all of his dirty little secrets. "My name is Amanda, and I will be your new physical therapist. May I come in?"

Joshua had never let a woman into his house without another person that he knew already there. Of course, Joshua was living a life of firsts, why would he stop now. Amanda began shifting her weight between her feet, probably trying to figure out what he was thinking. He finally opened the door and moved out of the way.

"Looks like you're moving well with the crutches," she seemed to be making small talk, but as soon as Joshua closed the door Amanda got right to it. "Okay look, I know you didn't want a female here because you didn't want the people of your community to think weird things were going on here, but hear me out." She paused to take a breath. "John told me he had been having some trouble convincing you and your family that the prosthetic was the way to go. I offered to come to help you ease your mind. See, I work with the prosthetics all the time. I'm not an actual physical therapist, you might say... really I just stock the closets and make sure the patients do well after the integration surgery but—"

"Get to the point." Joshua had had enough of the rambling. Amanda looked at him strangely for a minute, and then nodded.

"The point. Well, the point is, I want to help you and your family put your minds at ease about this decision to use this new prosthetic."

"I don't have a family."

"What?" Amanda looked confused by that statement.

"I don't need family to live. It's just me now. And I've already made up my mind that I want this prosthetic."

"Oh," she looked a little crestfallen. She had prepared a big speech and defense and it appeared as though she over-prepared. "But, just for the record, you do still have family right? They're not... dead or something?"

"To you, they might as well be." With that, Joshua hobbled toward the kitchen, effectively ending any form of conversation about his family. The last thing he wanted to talk about was what gave him so much pain. He took a couple glasses and a bottle of amber liquid and poured two small portions in each cup. He handed one of them to Amanda.

"What is this?"

"Scotch."

"Are we celebrating something?"

"The fact that my life is about to change." Joshua tilted his head and drank his portion in one swig. Amanda simply stared at hers as if she was debating.

"I'm sorry," she finally handed her glass back to Joshua. "I'm on the job." She smiled as if hoping that would ease the rejection of the drink. What she didn't realize is that Joshua intentionally poured her portion so that he could drink it when she refused. He had yet to see a nurse or physical therapist, or whatever they called themselves, drink any kind of alcohol unless it was purely by accident or they were tricked. Joshua didn't understand why you would want to trick someone into drinking alcohol—people either like it or they don't—but he had heard a lot of stories during his stay at the hospital.

Joshua finished her drink in one swig before setting the glasses down and asking her what he needed to do. It seemed as though Amanda was sent to convince and not necessarily to prepare for integration, so although she had little concerning her function this time, she promised the next time would be different.

In three days, someone would pick him up and take him to the clinic where he would be put under for surgery. There were pieces that had to be tapped into his spinal cord and nervous system so it was just like any other limb. As Joshua listened to Amanda talk, he knew he had made the right choice.

Maybe I can convince my parents of that when they see me with my new leg, he thought. He could only hope.

Amanda felt a little defeated leaving Joshua Miller's home. Something seemed off the entire time and she wasn't able to put her finger on it. The man seemed cordial enough for someone who was still dealing with the loss of his leg, but there was something else about him that seemed to make Amanda edgy.

Well, I have a while to figure it out, she thought to herself. *I'm stuck as his P.T. now, thanks to John and Dr. Zimmerman.*

The conversation only a few days prior had gone better than expected. Dr. Zimmerman had been debating throwing her into the field for some practice and figured who better to send his beloved Amanda to than a nice Amish family. What no one realized at the time was that this Amish family was falling apart at the seams and not even a limb could save it. So much could happen in the week of a patient of this caliber, and Amanda knew that, but something seemed different about this family. About Joshua.

Three days later, a few men came and picked Joshua up in a van much like Mr. Benjamin's and took him to the clinic for preparations. When they arrived, both Amanda and John were standing there waiting for him.

"Hello Joshua," John said as he opened the door. "It's good to see you here! Are you excited?"

Joshua simply nodded. There was no more need for words. Of course, it didn't help that everything seemed louder and brighter. Talking seemed to be difficult these days when that happened. Amanda noticed the flash of pain in his eyes and was more gentle with her tone and volume.

"Hi Joshua," she almost seemed to whisper, but that's all Joshua needed. She looked him in the eye and for the first time Joshua really noticed how blue her eyes were. They were a striking contrast to the deep brown of John's, who also had blond hair. If Joshua didn't know better, he would have thought they might be siblings.

As the van drove off, the trio walked into the clinic together. Amanda helped Joshua fill out the necessary paperwork while John went to the operating room to prepare with Dr. Zimmerman.

"How long will this take?" Joshua was sure Amanda had told him already, but he was so nervous he couldn't really function. She simply smiled understandingly and went through all of the information she had just gone through. Just as Joshua began to relax, John came to them and said they were ready. By then, he was ready as well.

Two months later

Joshua wasn't sure how Amanda kept managing to come back everyday when he would treat her like trash everyday. He just couldn't really function...

Amanda knew Joshua had been drinking. The only reason she kept coming back and didn't request that John take his patient back was because she knew that Joshua was better than that. She had seen him after the surgery. He was a completely different man. He was kind, funny, smart, and he knew how to hold a conversation.

Since coming home, Joshua went right back to his old habits. Amanda kept waiting for the right time to bring it up, but that next day might be the one. Joshua threatened her for the third time in as many days; he was getting worse. Every time he said something to her, it irritated her in some way. Did she have feelings for this broken Amish man who hadn't had contact with his family in almost four months?

The answer was a resounding yes. Because not only was he broken, he was attractive. Although he hadn't worked outside in almost six months, he still had a nice tan and chiseled skin with which his dark hair and soft, brown eyes flowed nicely. Amanda might have thought he was Native American if he hadn't told her some of his story about his family and growing up in the community. Something about this Amish "bad boy" really threw Amanda into a bind. John noticed it one day when she returned to the clinic one day.

"Aw, you have feelings for him," then he lowered his voice. "You have to be careful with that though. He is a patient. If you want to keep him as one, you need to make sure your feelings stay out of it."

Amanda already knew all of this, but it was good to have the reminder.

Joshua didn't understand Amanda. She was enigmatic as she was beautiful. He could tell that she knew about the drinking, but she hadn't said anything to him. Was she supportive of it? Did she hate it? Why was she being so silent about it all the time?

Joshua decided the next time he saw her, he would confront her. He wanted them to be totally open with each other.

The next day, when Amanda came to help Joshua with another rough day with the new prosthetic, he asked her the hard question.

"If you know about my drinking, why haven't you said anything to me?"

She was quiet for a few minutes as she avoided the question and focused instead on the physical therapy part of it. Regardless of what happened, in just under a week, Joshua would be done with physical therapy and they would never see each other again. He wasn't afraid to ask the question because he knew he would never see her again.

"Because I love you," she finally admitted. Joshua was taken aback. "I thought they were just feelings, but I realize now that I love you. I didn't say anything because I was trying to find the right words to say. You might think I have a way with words, but I really don't. Most conversations I start, I thought up on the way here from my house everyday. I can't imagine life without you, Joshua Miller. Even if I had to leave my dream job behind... I would do that for you." It was quiet between them for a few moments before Joshua spoke.

"I don't deserve your love."

"Is anyone deserving of the love they receive from another person? We learn how to love from the One Who created us, from God Himself. He loved without hardly ever receiving anything in return. No one who is loved ever deserves it. But that doesn't mean that we don't still give it. Joshua, you're still not talking to your family and it's been months. In fact, I don't even know what your family looks like if I needed to. For you to have no relationship with anyone in your family isn't right. You pushed them away, but for what? For alcohol? Because they upset you? Because you feel like you failed? Well guess what? Don't you think they feel like they failed? You were alone when you were in your accident! One of the biggest jobs for a parent is to keep their child safe. There is no greater failure for a parent than when they have to see their child get hurt and then reject all love from them."

By the time either of them realized Amanda was on a roll, it was too late to stop.

"You might think you're protecting people by keeping them out of your life, but really all you're doing is hurting yourself. Please Joshua..." she moved closer to him, inches away from his face. "Stop pushing me away." Without thinking about it, Joshua grabbed her face and pulled her in for a kiss. He had never kissed a woman before, but something about the way he did it and the feelings he got from it seemed right. Just like with the prosthetic, he knew Amanda was right. Not only in what she said, but in who she was and what she meant to him. He pulled her away to look into her eyes. There were tears in them.

"That was great... but do you really love me, Joshua?" She whispered so quietly, he almost missed what she said, but when he caught it his heart broke into a million pieces and he crumpled to the floor and wept. Amanda kneeled next to him and they just held each other and cried for a long while.

Joshua let it all out. All of the pain, the hurt, the feelings of anger toward the community, the feelings of betrayal against his family. He asked Amanda to pray with him to God to ask for forgiveness for everything that he had done and said. When they were finished, he felt really clean for the first time in a long time.

"There's still a few other things you need to fix before you can move on with your life... but we don't have to worry about that today." Amanda stood to leave.

"Wait!" Joshua was surprised at his sudden urgency. He pulled himself up so that they were standing toe to toe once again. "I want to fix that today."

Amanda looked at him for a moment. "Are you sure? That's going to be a hard wound to heal."

"Then it's the one I need to work on," Joshua said resolutely.

"Okay," Amanda grabbed her keys. "I don't care what you want to do, we're taking my car to get there." He smiled.

"I can agree to that."

Ten minutes later, Joshua and Amanda pulled up to Joshua's parents' house. Miriam and Samuel were on the front porch talking. When Miriam saw Joshua she jumped up and ran inside, leaving Samuel alone and confused.

"Hi there," Amanda called. Samuel simply waved, so Joshua made introductions. As soon as he finished, Miriam burst out of the house with the rest of the Miller clan on her heels. They all rushed Joshua so quickly that Amanda had to move out of the way to avoid being trampled. She moved to stand by Samuel while there was much crying from the family.

"How do you know the Miller's?" Amanda asked Samuel.

"I'm courting Miriam," he answered simply. "We're getting married in the spring."

"Congratulations," she smiled, then turned her attention back to the Miller's. After a few more minutes of hugs and tears, Joshua finally broke free.

"Mother, Father... I need to tell you something," he began. Mr. Miller put his hand on his eldest son's shoulder.

"No you don't, son. All you needed to say, anything you've done... it's been forgiven. It's done." His father smiled at him, and Joshua knew in that instant that anything he wanted to say didn't need to be said. But he had to do it for his sake.

"Well then let me tell you anyway. I went with the prosthetic and it's finally working like it's supposed to, thanks to Amanda." Joshua pointed to where she was standing as she waved awkwardly. He held her gaze for an extra moment before looking back at his parents. "But I gave into the sin of alcoholism. I pushed everyone away because I didn't want you all to see me as the failure that I am."

"Honey, we have *never* seen you as a failure," Mrs. Miller interjected. "We're just glad to have our son back." Joshua smiled, and Amanda realized he wasn't done.

"There's something else... this bit of news is a little harder to give." Joshua rubbed the back of his neck awkwardly. "I want to leave the Plain lifestyle." Miriam and James gasped, Samuel's eyes went wide, but Mr. and Mrs. Miller simply looked at each other and nodded.

Mrs. Miller explained, "When we saw you pull up with Amanda, we thought you had already."

"I don't think I could have left without saying goodbye to the people that brought me into this world and taught me everything I know about how to be a man of God." Tears filled Joshua's eyes again and he almost cursed because he promised himself he wouldn't cry. "I love Amanda, and she's shown me so much about how to live life. She's shown me a new perspective every time she's talked to me... and really she's the reason I'm even alive right now." He looked back at her and she had a mixed look of shock and love on her face. Joshua chuckled inwardly. "I know this seems like a bad time to be leaving right after making amends but—"

He was cut off from his mother crushing him into a hug.

"You just go and be the man you know God is calling you to be," she said as she pulled away.

"Wait," it was Amanda. "You—you're leaving now?" Joshua seemed confused by what was happening.

"Yes. The sooner, the better, right?" Amanda came down from the porch.

"No, not right. Joshua, your sister is getting married in the spring! If you excommunicate yourself now, you'll never be able to see her get married! No! You need to stay. At least until your sister gets married. But only if I get an invite." She had said that last sentence directly to Miriam who, until that point seemed the most devastated by her brother leaving. All you could see on her face in that moment was a smile.

"Anything to keep my brother here for a little while longer," Miriam sighed, relieved that he would be around to help with preparations.

"Besides," Amanda added. "It gives Joshua time to test out how well his leg would work in a Plain lifestyle." She looked at him and winked.

Over the next few months, Joshua and Amanda spent as much time as they could repairing relationships with the community and getting to know each other as individuals instead of as therapist and patient. John was less than excited about the sudden change in Joshua and Amanda's relationship, but Amanda realized it wasn't as sudden as she thought.

Once someone's true feelings are out in the open, everything happens very quickly. It's the journey to that point that seems the longest and the hardest... but it is the best journey because that is where true love is born.

Springtime, Miriam's wedding

Joshua was glad he waited until after the winter season to leave. Spring was always his favorite season growing up, and now it seemed like he was seeing all of the colors for the first time. With Amanda's help, Joshua had gotten off of all alcohol. He had repaired all relationships with the community and was even loved by all. He realized he had been too hard on them all in the beginning. It's not that they faked the love they had, it was that they didn't know how to show true love.

The preacher had asked Joshua if he wanted to take over the community's preacher position when he retired, but Joshua had made up his mind that he was leaving with Amanda the day after his sister's wedding.

"It's so beautiful," Amanda whispered beside him, just low enough that only he could hear it.

"Yes, you are," he whispered back. She gave him a scolding look as the preacher finished the vows with Samuel and Miriam.

"You may now kiss the bride."

Cheers and applause came from the open air as people stood from their seats to welcome the new union of Mr. and Mrs. Samuel Stoltzfus. Joshua was glad Amanda made him stay; he wasn't sure he ever would have forgiven himself if he left too early. If there was anyone he was going to miss, it was going to be Miriam.

In the receiving line, Joshua hugged Miriam extra tightly and whispered in her ear, "I love you Miriam. Be good for me. Write often." When they pulled back, there were tears in both of their eyes. They laughed.

"Ah, don't be such a softy," Miriam joked, before wiping her eyes and turning serious. "I love you, brother. You be good as well. It's a big world out there." He nodded.

"But I have a great woman and an even bigger God that will help me navigate." They both smiled.

"How did it go?" Amanda asked as they walked to her car. Joshua was quiet for a moment.

"Well."

"That's it? You're leaving your family forever and all you have to say about the last conversation with your sister is that it went 'well'?" Joshua laughed.

"No, but I need to process it before I can just go around telling people what happened. Let's move on to the next big adventure of our lives."

"You mean the first big adventure."

"For you maybe." They looked at each other for a minute before Amanda turned over the engine and drove away toward the city, leaving everything Joshua knew behind him.

I never thought my life would go this way, but I can't imagine it ending any other way.

For that, Joshua was glad. He didn't like having all of the answers anyway.

* 9 7 9 8 2 2 4 9 3 1 9 0 3 *